M000011775

LIVING SPRINGS PUBLISHERS PRESENTS:

STORIES THROUGH THE AGES
BABY BOOMERS PLUS
2022

Compiled and edited by:
Henry E. Peavler, Dan Peavler, and
Jacqueline Veryle Peavler

Introduction by: Henry Peavler and Dan Peavler

Short Stories by:
Joanne Guidoccio, Diane Lavin, Michael Jefferson, Emely Bennett,
Susan Evans, C. E. Reynolds, Carol Campbell, Rosemarie S. Perry,
Gerald Ryan, J. R. Reynolds, Alan Gartenhaus, Elaine Thomas,
Karen Ekstrom, Adele Evershed, Mary Ellen Fox, Ann Worrel

Each story in this collection is a work created from the imagination or experience of the author. The views expressed in the stories do not necessarily reflect the views of Living Spring Publishers LLP

Copyright 2022

by Living Springs Publishers LLP

Paperback ISBN: 978-1-953686-18-3
Paperback ISSN: 2770-0178
eBook ISBN: 978-1-953686-19-0
eBook ISSN: 2770-0194

All rights reserved including the right of reproduction in whole or in part in any form without written permission from the publisher

Living Springs Publishers

www.LivingSpringsPublishers.com

Cover design by Jacqueline Peavler

Dedicated to the ways we are alike, regardless of our differences.

Contents

Synopses

The Blizzard of '78: Diane Lavin's excellent relationship story wins 1st place in the 2022 edition of Stories Through the Ages Baby Boomers Plus. A blizzard is the setting. A reluctant mother facing her own demons must come to grips with the reality of a husband and daughter that she both loves and resents. The characters leap from the pages like the howling wind from the Blizzard of '78'.

Rounding Third: Author Elaine Thomas is the 2nd place prize winner in the 2022 edition of Stories Through the Ages Baby Boomers Plus. An unwitting love triangle with her dead brother's best friend and the young boy next door set the stage for a young woman ready to start a new stage of her life. A fantastic coming-of-age story.

Mouth Sewn Shut: As the only witness to the assault and abduction of her sister, Martha is under pressure to remember what happened. Mary Ellen Fox, the 3rd place prize winner in the 2022 edition of Stories Through the Ages Baby Boomers Plus, has given us a look inside the mind of a troubled young girl.

Jimmy's Swing: It is moving day from the family home and our heroine reminisces about her life with Jimmy while sitting on the swing he built for her. Emely Bennett has given us a poignant tale of moving on when life changes and an excellent surprise ending that makes sense after the fact.

Rightful Magic: A midwife and healer of the 16th century, who is running away from home, performs a good deed in a neighboring town. When things appear to go wrong, she is accused of witchcraft by the people she tried to help. A riveting story by Carol Campbell. Very creative and well written.

New Neighbors: It's 1996, and a young environmental consultant is intrigued by the mysterious new tenants in the office next door. Something is up in the sleepy little town of Helena, Montana and she is dying to find out what it might be. In her wildest imaginings, she could never have envisioned what the real story was and how it would light up the news media around the world. Author Karen Ekstrom has given us an excellent story.

Waiting Room: Henry and Lillis deal with the stress of waiting on the results of a biopsy while at the same time dealing with their two adult children. The successful daughter who has little time for them and the son who puts in the time but not the effort. Susan Evans has given us a great story of family relations.

The Blessings of Grasshoppers: The grasshoppers used as bait to fish become the food needed for survival when a virus rampages the world. Adele Evershed has written a fantastic story of love, family, and the basic instinct to survive whatever the cost.

The Outing: A man gets up the courage to visit a gay bar. We don't want to give the plot away, but Alan Gartenhaus has written a story that made us chuckle at the end.

Between Heaven and Earth: Frugalista, a superstar angel from the Depression era, reluctantly agrees to help boomer women and their older sisters deal with the after-effects of the 2008 recession. Her first client is a divorced, unemployed woman who has just received a cancer diagnosis. An inspiring and entertaining tale from Joanne Guidoccio.

Curse of the Cane Man: A newly hired detective investigates the disappearance of some local people. His inquiries turn up more than a simple tale of abduction. A story of intrigue by Michael Jefferson. Beautifully written and crafted with more than its share of gripping revelations.

An American in Paris: Rosemarie S. Perry shares her eye-opening month-long trip through Europe in 1972 as a solo traveler. It makes you wonder, was I ever that young and naïve, and would I do it again?

Migrations: A Vietnam veteran and Native American struggle as lonely outsiders in their own birthlands in this story set in the 1970s. A tale of the times by C. E. Reynolds.

A Night in a Rural Town: A man has car trouble in a rural area and must spend the night. From the moment he arrives he is treated to the friendliness of people in a small town. Through a chance visit with the local rancher, he enjoys an evening of fine country cooking and hospitality. A heartwarming story by J. R. Reynolds.

A Saturday Night: A simpler time when kids played outside. A group of boys decide to "go harvesting" from a Jewish sukkah, which puts them in danger from local gangs and on the radar of the local police. A very entertaining story by Gerald Ryan of how appearances aren't always what they seem.

Dodge City: A coming-of-age story about a young man who draws a low number in the Vietnam draft lottery. Rick receives conflicting advice from his family, his friends, and a former military man who tells him...'Don't Go!' What should he do? Excellent story by Ann Worrel

Introduction

We at Living Springs Publishers are pleased to share stories from the winners of our "Stories Through the Ages Baby Boomers Plus 2022" short story contest. For the second year in a row the contest has been chosen as one of the best writing contests by Reedsy. As in previous years we received submissions from successful, award-winning authors from all parts of the United States and around the world. Many of the authors are established with a lifetime of literary achievements, while others have just began writing in their retirement.

Living Springs Publishers hope that we can find commonality and peace in the world. An Irish proverb states, "It is in the shelter of each other that people live." We shouldn't have to wait for a war or crisis for us to find our similarities. The stories in this book show that we are all much more alike than different. Our authors transport moments in time from their own unique experiences into stories that capture the reader's interest, curiosity and awareness.

Memories are our own personal stories. The talented

group of writers that make up this extraordinary book have taken great pains to share their creativity and imaginations. Every story, idea, or thought we share with the world affects it, no matter how small or trivial we think it might be. Talent and genius are often lost forever for the lack of courage. We thank all those who had the daring to offer their stories for everyone to read.

The Blizzard of '78
By Diane Lavin

Vivian balanced her coffee, toast, the morning paper, and a pack of Virginia Slims on a small tray and used her foot to close the door to the study. She set the tray down, removed the cover from her Selectric, and offered a nodding glance out her window to Lake Erie, a volatile body of water churning and frothing that morning as the blizzard moved in. Vivian wasn't bothered by news of another blizzard; Cleveland already had 20 inches of snow on the ground. She sipped her coffee and pulled her notes from the day before. Though the wind roared like rams bashing heads, Vivian focused on her work, an essay series for *The Plain Dealer*.

Downstairs, Vivian's husband Richard packed their daughter's lunchbox while the nine-year-old tilted her cereal bowl to slurp the remaining milk. He bundled her up and tied her scarf, then opened the front door, allowing an icy gust of wind and snow to choke the vestibule. "My God, Libby," he said. "I should drive you today."

Libby shook her head. "It's like Dorothy's cyclone." They watched *The Wizard of Oz* the past Friday night. "I'm brave like the lion," she growled.

"Yes, you are." Richard kissed the top of her pom-pom hat and sent her out. He watched her lunge to reach the mailman's footprints, her scarf flapping uselessly. *Adorable,* he thought, then packed his briefcase and called a goodbye to Vivian upstairs.

Libby arrived late to school as did other students whose parents, like Richard, let them face the storm, or who, like Vivian, never drove their children to school.

The storm intensified throughout the morning, hurtling itself against Libby's classroom windows and drawing the fourth graders away from their desks. They placed their hands, foreheads, and noses on the skin-numbing glass, mesmerized as snow and ice engaged in a violent dance, barreling sideways across the playground, piling in drifts against the fence.

"It's a twister," Libby said. Her classmates nodded. Every one of them had stayed up the previous Friday to watch the celebrated annual airing.

The principal announced that school would dismiss early. "Your parents are being called," Miss Henley said to a cheering class. "Until then, everyone should work on their math sheets."

No one worked on their math sheets. They guessed which mothers would come, though a few boys boasted they wanted to walk home. At dismissal, Libby scrutinized the line of cars, each with someone else's mom, each kept running and warm. She huddled inside her coat and began the trek home.

Downtown, a barrage of ice slammed into Richard's 12th-floor office windows. The onslaught drew his attention from the brief on his desk. He went to the window and looked down but could not see the street.

His secretary poked her head in. "The firm is closing early, Mr. Benton."

"Thank you, Mary. Drive safely."

"You, too, Mr. Benton."

Richard's commute northeast along the lake guaranteed a dreadful ride home. He packed his briefcase and phoned Vivian to say he was leaving early. She didn't pick up.

Neither did Vivian answer the phone when Libby's school called. She was concentrating on photographs of prominent Cleveland women of the '60s, the inspiration for her current series. She wrote exactingly about a time of civil unrest when fierce and independent women carved a place for themselves in jurisprudence, politics, journalism. It was before life sidelined Vivian from what she might have had: recognition, a decent salary, and career opportunities outside hometown Cleveland.

Vivian had commuted to college where she met Richard. They married a month before graduation, deciding to hold off starting a family since Richard was headed to law school and Vivian to graduate school in journalism. That summer, however, Vivian learned she was pregnant, and they agreed she would postpone entering in the fall. The postponement became permanent, and the thought still pinched deep in her chest. Why had she agreed to wait? Was she not confident or independent enough to have a child and a career?

She didn't discuss her regret with her parents, who felt she had everything a woman could want: a husband who loved and provided for her, a house, a child. She didn't talk to Richard either, who had advanced over the years to partner. At each step, they toasted his success, and after each toast, Vivian climbed into their bed feeling smaller and emptier.

Enough, she thought. *Focus.* She lifted a photo of Francis Bolton who had four children and served in the U.S. House of Representatives, and one of Dorothy Fuldheim who had a child and became the first female television news anchor. Margaret Hamilton raised a son on her own and rose to fame as an actress, which Vivian mentioned to Libby and Richard when the opening credits to *The Wizard of Oz* rolled across the screen.

"We know, Mom," Libby said dismissively. She curled up on the couch and made Richard promise not to let her fall asleep this time. He promised and set the pan of Jiffy Pop between them. Vivian paused, then headed upstairs.

***

With eight blocks left, Libby plodded along. The storm was so fierce, she couldn't tell when she was stepping off a curb. She struggled to be brave though the wind pushed her down, stifled her breathing, and chapped her face.

A blast of prickly ice sent the hall rug flying when Libby finally burst into the house. Her eyelashes were caked with snow, her legs throbbing and flaming red. She shook her mittened hand and screamed, "I hate my life!" But it wasn't that she hated her life. She hated her mother who looked up from her typewriter and wondered, *Is it 4:00 already?*

Libby kicked the wall trying to get her boots off. She growled like a beast and whipped her braids around to let fly ice and snow.

"Elizabeth Louise, for God's sakes," Vivian said.

Libby yanked off her coat, stomped on it, and continued stomping up each stair where she slammed her bedroom door and flung herself on the bed. She vowed to hate her mother forever, then curled under the covers for warmth.

Vivian shrugged and dutifully made hot chocolate.

"Don't come in!" Libby shouted.

"It has marshmallows," Vivian said coaxingly.

"Everyone else's mom came. You never came!"

"What?" Vivian tilted her head. Had she missed a program at school? "Libby?"

"Go away," Libby shouted, elongating each syllable.

Back in the kitchen, Vivian dumped the hot chocolate down the sink. *She's impossible* she thought and returned to her study, lit a cigarette, and finally noticed what was happening outside. She turned on the radio to hear weatherman Dick Goddard describe a once-in-a-century storm. *Everyone else's mom came,* Vivian thought. *Was I supposed to pick her up?*

Vivian's stomach sickened. Familiar, this misery, her daughter's disappointment in her. Of course, she should have picked her up. But how was she to know? *I did make hot chocolate,* she thought, which Libby had rejected, which Vivian took personally.

After a long draw on her cigarette, Vivian lost herself in the twisted world outside her window. The ferocity made her heart pound. *Once-in-a-century,* she thought. She moved the current project aside, stubbed out the cigarette, and turned her attention to documenting the storm.

In the next room, Libby stopped shivering and

climbed out of bed. She surveyed the lake and sky. They were frothy, dirty yellows, opaline white, slate grey with hints of purple. Libby knew this blizzard. She liked that it was fierce. She pushed her desk to the window, swept aside yesterday's drawings, and set to work sketching the enemy outside.

Texture, color, anything scratchy, plush, or slick had always delighted Libby. As a small child, she sat in puddles and gleefully spread mud up and down herself. She finger-painted past the easel and onto the walls and raided low cupboards for containers to spill and spread in designs across the kitchen floor.

Vivian bemoaned the mess and took no delight in Libby's artistic expression, which grew more sophisticated. Richard taped sketches on the refrigerator which Vivian tolerated for a time and then took down. When Richard bought special pencils, paints, and paper for Libby, Vivian called it frivolous. "She should be learning to read and write, not draw," she said, raising a sensitive topic.

In first grade, Libby struggled to trace the letters until finally, her feet planted and arms crossed, she refused to practice them at all. Vivian told Richard to read more to Libby, which both loved, but when he urged her to read, Libby used the pictures to make up the story. If Vivian insisted she stick with what was written, Libby would throw the book across the room. Once Vivian shouted, "I simply cannot have a child who doesn't read and write!"

Libby had fled crying. Richard told Vivian to calm down. "She's trying," he said and went to comfort her.

Moments like these prompted Vivian to call her older sister. "I swear, Carol, between her bull-headedness and him spoiling her, I don't know who to slap first."

Carol advised Vivian to ask Libby's teachers. They were experts, after all.

"Oh, I did," Vivian said sarcastically. '"Students learn to read at different rates, Mrs. Benton. Look how advanced her drawings are.' Or my favorite: 'Maybe if you spent more time with her on homework, Mrs. Benton.' It's infuriating, Carol. I am not the mother who bakes cookies and helps with homework. I'm just not."

***

That evening, after a harrowing drive home, Richard

abandoned the car when it got stuck in the driveway and trudged, cursing, to the back door where he spent another quarter-hour shoveling sufficiently to force it open. Swallowing his frustration, he called out in a measured voice, "I'm home. Everyone here good?"

No one responded. He sighed, gathered wood from the stack against the garage, started a fire, poured himself a scotch, and went upstairs. "Who wants dinner?" he asked.

"Hi, Dad!" said Libby. She spread out her sketches of the storm, shades of white in swirls, a child whose scarf was blowing away. One sketch, however, of a woman in a black cape lying in the snow, she turned over.

"Is this you?" Richard asked, referring to the child with the scarf.

Libby nodded. "I lost it."

"Your scarf?"

"Uh-huh."

"You lost it on the way to school? I should have given you a ride."

"Walking home."

"You walked home? By yourself? Mom didn't pick

you up?"

Libby shrugged. "It's okay, Dad. I didn't think she would."

Richard shook his head but held his tongue.

***

For three days Cleveland was shut down. City plows moved mountains of white into larger mountains of white. Streets were lined with cars buried above their hoods. Dog owners struggled to take their dogs out to pee.

Many families played board games, baked brownies, or watched T.V. together. The Bentons did not do these things. It wasn't until dinner that the three shared time as a family.

"We're in for another couple of days at least," Richard said. "Tomorrow, let's build a snowman."

"Dad," said Libby, offended.

"What? If I'm not too old, then you aren't either."

Libby shoveled a forkful of spaghetti into her mouth.

"We should check on our neighbors. See if anyone lost power," Vivian said. "We have room if they can get here."

Libby rolled her eyes.

"What?" Vivian said.

"Nothing. It's nice that you think about other people."

"Enough, young lady!" Vivian said. "I'm sorry I didn't pick you up, but you're fine now, so can we please finish dinner in peace?" She polished off her wine and Richard rose to clear the plates.

Then the power went out.

**

"Libby, get the flashlights from the hall closet," said Vivian. "Richard, do we have enough wood? Bring down a bunch of blankets. We'll set up in front of the fireplace."

Libby saluted and scampered up the stairs. Vivian pushed the living room furniture aside. Richard fetched armloads of wood. That night, the family camped by the fire.

"Who wants to hear a scary story?" asked Richard.

"Dad," said Libby, with her most offended voice.

Richard shrugged. "Vivian?"

"Sure. Why not."

Libby put her head in her hands as Richard said, "The last man on Earth sat in a room. Suddenly, there was a knock on the door."

"Dad!" said Libby. "Stop."

Vivian laughed. "I love that two-liner."

Libby stared in disbelief. "Who's the kid here?"

Vivian playfully tossed a pillow at Libby which she threatened to toss back, then kept for herself. Soon the three settled in, blankets above and below them, smelling the crackling, spitting fire, listening as ice pelted the roof.

Power returned before dawn. Vivian and Richard woke and breathed sighs of relief. They looked at Libby curled up with a dozen stuffed animals.

"She's beautiful," whispered Richard.

"When she's sleeping."

"Oh, come on. Don't say that."

Vivian shrugged.

"Viv, what is this all about?" asked Richard.

Libby, waking, caught the pressing tone in her father's voice and kept her eyes shut. She held still, like an alert rabbit.

"It's nothing, Richard. Just, you know."

"I don't know," he said.

Vivian took and released a deep breath. "We weren't ready, Richard. We weren't." She fought off tears as she nodded toward Libby.

Richard, puzzled, said, "Are you talking about nine years ago? I thought we were past all that."

"Richard, deciding to wait before starting a family and then learning a month later we're having a baby doesn't change a person's feelings just like that."

"I guess it did for me."

"Well, I wasn't ready," Vivian said softly. "I was 22, Richard. I wanted time, a chance to have my own life."

Richard tilted his head. "What are you saying? You don't like the life we have? Or is it me you regret marrying?"

Libby held her breath.

Vivian shrugged and told Richard about a letter from her college roommate. "She's in New York. She's working for *The New York Review of Books*."

"Okay," Richard said, unsure of the point.

"She's got a career, Richard. In New York. She made it."

"And you think you haven't?" He swept his arm to include himself, the house, Libby.

Vivian's eyes fixed on Libby.

"You think because of her?" whispered Richard. "Viv, that's – I don't even know what to call it."

"Horrible. Selfish. Immature."

"Sad," said Richard. "And painful, to be honest."

"Well, it's not as though I don't love her. Of course, I love her." She shook her head. "Forget it."

Libby struggled to breathe. Trapped between the falsehood that she was asleep and the truth of her mother's words, she rolled over to hide her tears.

The three spent the morning apart. Vivian kept the radio on and heard that the wind chill was 30 degrees below zero. Thousands of trees had blown down, miles of power lines were snapped across the city, the death toll was rising. It felt fitting to write about a disaster.

Down the hall, Libby drew, pressing on the pencils so hard they broke. To the drawing with the woman in black she added a broomstick, and above her wrote, "the wich is ded."

By lunchtime, Richard, who'd given up shoveling the

car out, knocked lightly and entered Libby's room. She quickly covered the drawing and bent over her sketchbook.

"Dad, I'm busy."

"Okay," he said and closed the door.

Libby's shoulders sank as her father left. She shoved the drawings away, folded her arms on the desk, put her head onto them, and cried.

Late that afternoon, the phone rang. "It's Carol," Richard said to Vivian who was heading downstairs for more coffee.

She took the receiver. "We did. Did you?" she asked. "No, it came back on sometime during the night."

Vivian took the phone and her coffee into the breakfast nook. Libby came down to make a sandwich and stepped over the cord running across the kitchen floor.

"Who's Mom talking to?"

"Aunt Carol," said Richard.

Libby pulled peanut butter from the cupboard. Richard handed her the strawberry jam. "Come sit by the fire with me," he offered, and Libby nodded.

"No, that's what's so hilarious," Vivian said, her back turned. "She bursts in screaming, 'I hate my life.' Carol, she looked like an iced-over snowman, and she was only out there a few minutes."

Libby scrunched her face. *A few minutes?*

"I know, right? She hates her life. If she was 15, I'd get it. But nine?"

Libby pressed on the top piece of bread until strawberry jam squeezed out the sides.

"In her room mostly," Vivian continued. "Drawing, of course. What else?" She waved at Libby, and said, "It's Aunt Carol on the phone. You want to say 'hi?'"

Libby shook her head. Vivian shrugged. "Oh, my God, Carol. Are you kidding? Monopoly? Richard's done nothing but shovel and Libby's practicing being a pouty teenager."

Libby slammed her hand on the counter. "Mom!" she shouted and ran upstairs.

Richard returned to the kitchen. "What happened?"

"Hold on, Carol." Vivian covered the receiver and whispered to Richard, "I think Libby wants us to play Monopoly."

Richard frowned.

"It's nothing, Richard. And don't go up there. If she wants to have a tantrum, let her."

Richard ignored Vivian's directive and went upstairs. This time Libby didn't hide any drawings.

"What is this?" he asked, lifting the sketch of the woman in black lying in the snow.

Libby threw the charcoal pencil across the room. "Her," she said.

"Your mother? Why?"

"She told Aunt Carol what happened, and she got the whole thing wrong."

Richard sat on the bed and patted the space next to him. Libby plopped down and leaned against his side. "So, tell me what Mom got wrong."

Libby launched into an animated account of walking home the day before. "We left school at 2:30. I didn't get home until 4! She told Aunt Carol I was only outside for a few minutes! And then she laughed about it."

"Did Mom know school let out at 2:30?"

"I don't know. Miss Henley said they were calling our parents."

Richard remembered calling home about that time.

Libby looked at the floor. "And Dad, I heard you this morning."

"This morning?"

"I faked being asleep, but I heard you and Mom. I heard her say she never wanted to have me, and I heard you say that was really sad." She burst into tears.

Vivian, who had tiptoed up the stairs for her cigarettes, made it halfway, heard the commotion, and tried to tiptoe down, but the creaking steps revealed her presence. Richard called out that she might as well come in.

She hesitated. She didn't have the strength. She didn't see the point. She bolted to her study but stubbed her toe on the top step. "Shit," she said. She swiped the pack of cigarettes from her desk and hurried down the stairs.

Richard gathered his resolve. He took Libby gently by the shoulders and said, "We have to talk to Mom."

Libby twisted away. "I'm not talking to her. And don't you tell her."

"We have to talk to her." He gathered the recent

drawings. "Come on," he said, nodding to the door. "I'll do the talking."

Libby trudged behind her father down the stairs and into the kitchen. Vivian sat in the breakfast nook with a glass of wine.

"Oh, Christ," she said, trapped in the small space. "What am I guilty of now?"

"We need to talk, Viv."

Vivian pulled out a cigarette, gave it two taps on the small table, lit it, and took a long draw.

Richard sat down, but Libby remained standing with her chin to her chest and her hair in her face.

"Oh, for God's sakes, Libby. I'm not that scary, am I?"

Libby didn't answer, so Richard began. "Viv, we love you-"

Vivian stared him down. She took another draw and blew the smoke across the table. Richard waved it away. Libby looked up with a scowl.

"What?" Vivian barked. "You have something to say?"

Richard opened his mouth, but Vivian cut him off.

"No. Let her tell me. You tell me, Libby. What horrible thing have I done now?"

Richard made a third attempt.

"Shut up, Richard. Stop rescuing her."

"Mom!" said Libby. "You stop. Dad's only trying to help." She clenched her hands, her teeth, her eyes. She grabbed the drawings from her father, ripped them one at a time, and crumpled the pieces. "This is what I want you to know, Mom," she said shoving them into the trash. "And also, I heard you talking this morning when you thought I was sleeping. I heard you, okay?"

Vivian gasped. She turned to Richard with begging eyes.

"She heard everything," he said softly.

"Oh my God. Oh my God." Vivian reached out to her.

Libby stared at her mother's hand. She didn't want it. She didn't trust it. "The witch is dead," she mumbled and walked away.

Vivian broke down. She let Richard guide her into the living room where they sat together as early evening set in.

"I'm a horrible, horrible person. I'm a horrible mother."

"Viv, you love Libby. It's not too late to fix things with her."

"What if it is?" Vivian asked. She collapsed onto Richard's shoulder. "And what about me? I never even went to graduate school."

Richard separated from Vivian to face her. "You want to go back to school?"

"Do you think I'm too old? Do you think it's too late?"

"I don't know, Viv. I don't want to discourage you if that's what you really want. But how would that work?"

"I don't know. I just know I want more than this," Vivian said waving at the room.

"A career."

"Yes, and a name for myself and all the things you have."

Richard lifted one brow. "It's not so great, Viv. Trust me."

"I still want it. And I'm not giving up this time."

"Giving up?"

"On myself. I'm not giving up on myself this time."

Richard rose and poured himself a drink, then sat with his arm around Vivian, thinking and stroking her hair as she let her body relax.

***

Sometime before dawn, Vivian peeled herself off the couch. Richard was asleep, the house quiet. She went to the kitchen and picked out the torn drawings from the trash. Piecing them together, she saw the blizzard come to life. She felt herself inside the storm, and it made her heart race. She saw the woman in black and read 'the wich is ded.' She imagined Margaret Hamilton's threatening voice.

"Oh, Libby," she said aloud. "I'm the wicked witch, and you're just a little girl who wants a home."

Instinctively she reached for a cigarette, then stopped as her mouth filled with saliva. She raced to the powder room in time to throw up in the toilet. Cold and shivering on the tile floor, her insides floating in the water, she used the sink to pull herself up and rinsed out her mouth. A bleached face stared back from the mirror.

"Enough," she said to the wretched woman staring at

her.

***

The snow glistened as the sun rose. The blizzard had moved on. Vivian brought the sketches to Libby's room and stood over her sleeping daughter. She leaned down and moved a curl from Libby's face; the sketches fell to the floor. "I'm sorry," she whispered. "I am so sorry."

Gently, Vivian lifted the corner of the blanket and slipped into Libby's bed.

Meteorologists classified the blizzard as explosive cyclogenesis, a bomb cyclone, the result of a polar jet stream racing down from Canada and colliding with a subtropical jet stream moving up from the Gulf of Mexico. It was the worst, though not the final storm of Cleveland's winter of '78.

Diane Lavin

Diane grew up in a small town south of Cleveland, Ohio, when kids walked to school regardless of the weather. She decided in first grade to be a teacher and treasures the decades dedicated to her students. She has three grown children and four gorgeous grandchildren. She and her husband met in middle school and are approaching their 50th wedding anniversary. *The Blizzard of '78* is her first completed short story.

Rounding Third
By Elaine Thomas

The batter drove a solid hit deep into right field, pushing runners on first and second forward. Billy headed into third, arms and legs pumping. Mo looked toward home, where all she really saw was Ray.

Billy glanced at her, questioning whether or not to keep going. She signaled him on, knowing he could score the run needed to tie the game—with players left on first and second for a possible win.

Billy was a gentle, red-haired kid, with a shy smile and adorable dimples. Mo had known the boy his entire life. Their families lived in the same neighborhood and attended the same Episcopalian church. She could remember when he was born.

That he'd developed a crush on Mo this summer was obvious; he followed her around the church camp like a puppy. She felt protective toward him. She knew what it was like to imagine you could be old enough for someone when you just weren't. She even gave Billy one of her brother Denny's old baseball gloves and worked overtime with the boy to improve his game. He was a great kid.

Mo realized her mistake as soon as Billy rounded third. Running like a bat out of hell, he still wasn't fast enough to beat the fielder's throw to home. Penned between the catcher and third baseman, he was easily tagged out.

Mo had hoped to make Billy a hero of the game, the final one played on the last day of camp, a game that determined a full year's worth of bragging rights. Instead, she'd set him up. He was the third out in the top of the ninth by a team down one run. Game over. Cheering wildly, the winners rushed toward the plate to celebrate with chest bumps and fist pumps.

Billy maintained his composure as his team lined up and shook the winners' hands. As both teams left the field, she watched him drop his head. She felt a little like crying herself.

From behind the plate, Ray jogged down the third-base line to where Mo stood.

"Tough play."

"I feel bad! I shouldn't have waved him on."

"Aw, come on, third-base coaches make judgment calls. Not your fault the kid couldn't make the run in time. Besides, part of our job here is to toughen them up a little."

"Welcome to the 1980s," she smiled. "You do know it's ok nowadays for boys to be sensitive?"

Ray laughed. "Hey, aren't you leaving for college tomorrow? Got time for dinner tonight? We haven't really had a chance to talk all summer."

"Long as you're paying." Her tone was playful, but so many questions popped into her head. Like a date? Or just two old friends hanging out? Did he still think of her only as Denny's baby sister?

"Great, meet you at Hazel's around seven-thirty. Right now, I'm going for a run, work up an appetite." Ray turned and jogged away. He peeled off his umpire's shirt as he ran, dropping the shirt on the ground as he passed by home plate. Muscles rippled down both sides of his back.

Mo watched until he was out of sight. As she stood there, she was unaware of Billy observing from a distance.

Nobody runs like Ray Porter, she thought. Shoulders back, chest out, smooth strides of his long legs. Like everything about Ray, the way he ran was perfect. Mo had watched him run and loved him, and his perfection, pretty much her whole life.

As kids, her big brother and his best friend taught Mo to play both softball and baseball. Amazingly patient, neither Denny nor Ray seemed to mind the little girl following them around. It must've been annoying at times. *Then again,* she thought, *who wouldn't appreciate such constant adoration?*

Not that admiration was in short supply anywhere in the charmed lives of Raymond Porter, Jr., and Denton Lawson III. Respectively the sons of a Presbyterian minister and an attorney, the boys were hometown heroes in that particular way known only to handsome, high-achieving, athletic boys from prominent families in small southern towns.

Fleet-footed Ray played shortstop, with sure-handed Denny at first. Both made All Conference their junior, and senior years. They were the closest of friends, tighter than most brothers. They rarely argued, not even over girls; Denny tended to date blondes, while Ray chose pretty brunettes. They graduated the year before Mo started high school.

Neither fleet of foot nor sure of hand, she played third base on the girls' softball team. Thanks to Denny and Ray she did well because she knew the fundamentals better than most.

~   ~   ~

"Is that you, Maureen?" her father called out from his home office.

"Yes, Daddy, it's me, where's Mama?"

"Some kind of meeting at the church."

No surprise, either way. Since the loss of his only son and namesake, her father seemed to stop working only when he slept. Her mother seized every excuse to be out of the house these days.

She really couldn't blame them. But for a moment, just one moment, Mo let herself remember what things had been like before Denny's accident, before omnipresent grief hung over the house.

Driving home for Christmas break his freshman year

at State, his proud father's alma mater, the perfect son hit a patch of black ice just as he headed downslope onto a bridge. A bridge that he never made it across. At times Mo felt as if both her parents' lives had flickered out at that same moment, all light gone from their eyes. Neither had felt fully present to her since.

She quickly pushed these memories away.

"Daddy, I'm going to meet Ray Porter at Hazel's for dinner. Ok?"

"Of course, honey. Please give him our regards. Just don't forget what a big day tomorrow is. We want to leave early to get you to campus on time."

"Yes, sir."

For his eighteenth birthday, their parents gave Denny a brand-new SUV. They chose the vehicle in part for safety; the tragedy lay in a top-heavy design that made it difficult to control once it skidded. After what happened, her parents refused to buy, even to allow, Mo her own car. They insisted they would drive her to begin her freshman year at St. Stephen, less than an hour from home, even though she was only weeks away from eighteen.

She ran up the stairs to her room. Nothing she saw in her closet seemed right for tonight. Everything looked like a little kid's clothes. She was in no mood to be thought of as a kid.

Around age seven or eight, Mo decided Ray Porter was "the one". In the ensuing decade, her devotion never wavered, despite Ray's apparent indifference to that aspect of their relationship...AND despite the best efforts of boys her own age. She dated, even went steady a couple of times, but she never let things go beyond a certain point. None of them held any long-lasting appeal. None of them were Ray. Compared to him, guys her age seemed immature. It became even easier to dismiss them once she was the girl whose brother failed to make it home. They all acted as if she were somehow breakable because Denny died.

Tomorrow would begin a new phase in her life, but tonight Mo hoped to confirm once and for all, one way or the other, her long-held expectations of who she could be. She gave up on the closet's contents and opened one of her already packed suitcases. She pulled out her slinkiest green top, a rich jade color she knew set off both her eyes and her tanned skin. She paired it with her favorite pair of snug jeans.

"Bye, Daddy," she yelled over her shoulder as the screen door slapped shut behind her.

~ ~   ~

Owned and operated by a local family, Hazel's had been an institution in town since long before the arrival of any competing fast-food chains. Red leather and chrome reflected the relaxed decor and attitude of a bygone era but refreshed and updated. Prices remained reasonable, patrons remained loyal, and more importantly, the food remained exceptional. The restaurant drew families as well as young people and tended to be packed at all meals.

Ray got there before Mo and snagged an empty booth near the back.

He looked forward to catching up with Mo and hearing more about her college plans. She suddenly seemed so grown-up. The little girl who had followed Denny and him around was always a cute kid, but she had become a young woman who seemed more of a peer these days. A very pretty peer, he acknowledged, but his intense reactions to her were confusing. He wanted to be near her because he wanted to feel close to Denny. At the same time, when he looked at her, he felt the pain of Denny's loss.

Ray had always known Mo had a crush on him. He knew it the same way he knew most females found him attractive. But she was Denny's kid sister, which put her in an altogether different category. She would never be just a girl. He wouldn't do anything that might inadvertently hurt her. He purposely kept distance between them all summer, but felt safe enough inviting her to join him for dinner the night before she left for college.

When Mo entered the restaurant she looked to her left and spotted Ray. Had she looked to the right she would have seen Billy seated there, eating dinner with his parents.

She slid into the booth across from Ray. As she did, he stood; it struck her as both gentlemanly and an oddly old-fashioned gesture.

"Wow, look at you, little girl," he said, eyebrows raised.

Fresh-scrubbed, wearing a blue button-down shirt that matched the shade of his eyes, Ray looked great. He looked so good that she decided to ignore the "little girl" comment and just take the compliment.

He handed her a menu, as if either of them needed one at Hazel's, and asked, "What do you want to eat?"

They talked as they ate, the standard burgers and fries, with Ray eager to hear her expectations of college and willing to share any wisdom gathered during his three years at Tech. They talked about his plans after graduation; her thoughts on potential majors; how much bigger the world was than their small hometown. They didn't mention Denny, not even once.

"It's already dark," Ray said, after paying their bill. "Come on, I'll drive you home."

"Ok," she hesitated, then added, "but I don't want to go home yet. Can we just drive around for a while? You know, look the place over one last time before I leave tomorrow?"

He glanced at her, then shrugged. "Sure, jump in," he said, holding open the passenger-side door of his red Z28 convertible.

~ ~   ~

They rode through town twice, up then back down the main drag. That took only a few minutes, so Ray drove by her daddy's law firm and circled past First Presbyterian, where his own daddy was minister. He pulled into the parking lot at the high school, a squat one-story, flat-roofed building.

"Proud member of the class of 1978," he said.

"Proud 1981 graduate," she responded.

They both laughed.

They had pretty much done the entire tour of town, so Ray headed out toward the river. He pulled into a secluded spot, with the car facing the water. The moon's light shimmered on the surface. He had parked there many times but assumed Mo wouldn't be familiar with the spot. He switched off the engine, then flipped the key forward just enough to keep the radio on.

He reached past Mo to push the button to open the glove compartment. His hand accidentally brushed across her thigh. He fumbled around in the glove compartment and pulled out a joint and lighter. He fired up the joint, took a toke, and passed it to Mo. Within minutes they were both not just stoned, but totally shitfaced.

Mo couldn't believe the quality of sound coming through the car's speakers. Even in open air, with the convertible top down, music surrounded her. She relaxed, feeling more comfortable than she could remember at any time during the past couple of years. Ray felt safe, like home.

She sat with her knees pulled up into the seat, her back leaning against the door. She couldn't take her eyes off Ray's hands. They were beautiful, strong hands with long, sensitive fingers, thumbs with squared bottoms that stood out from his palms.

Ray lolled in the far corner of his seat, head laid back atop the door. He gazed up at the stars.

"Do you think Denny's somewhere up there looking down at us?" he asked in a slow, stoned voice.

Mo gave no answer. She couldn't stop staring at his hands.

Ray slowly rolled his head forward enough to look directly at her.

"I'm sorry! You know I miss him, too, don't you?"

She nodded, then reached over and took his hand, examining it closely for a moment. She looked up at him and they began to kiss.

Things escalated quickly. They were both partially undressed, when Ray heard the raucous opening notes of "Paradise by the Dashboard Light." *Bat Out of Hell* had played constantly throughout the spring of his and Denny's senior year of high school and into that summer. He knew every word of every song on the album. He tried to ignore the lyrics, but Meat Loaf's big voice belting out "We were barely seventeen and we were barely dressed" suddenly struck him as hilarious. That song, with those words, "Do you love me? Will you love me forever?" That crazy interlude with the baseball announcer describing a squeeze play between third and home.

He pulled away from Mo, retreating against the door on his side of the car, sat there and laughed. As stoned as he was, he couldn't stop laughing.

Maybe Denny had been watching. Maybe his own conscience, which had never bothered him before with a girl, finally caught up to him. He had been raised right; it was bound to happen sooner or later. Of all the songs to hear at that moment. Mo *was* seventeen. He felt sure she was a virgin. He was not about to take a chance on destroying the life that lay ahead of her. Or his own life.

He tried to get it together enough to apologize. He wanted to explain that it was the song and his own actions that had reduced him to a giggling mess.

"Mo, I'm sorry...."

He looked at her and took it all in, her disheveled appearance, the tears running down her cheeks, flowing from mascara-smudged eyes with huge pupils.

He pulled on his shirt and turned the ignition key.

"Mo, I'm taking you home."

They were both silent the entire way. Still stoned, Ray stared at the road ahead, concentrating on driving. From the corner of his eye he saw Mo button and straighten her clothes. Then, with arms crossed and head down, she withdrew into herself.

When they got to Mo's, the house was dark. *Good,* he thought, *please let her parents be asleep.* He pulled into the driveway. As soon as the car stopped, she flung the door open. Ray reached over and grabbed her wrist.

"Wait," he said. "I can't stand thinking I've upset you, Mo. You know how much you matter to me."

She pulled her hand free, slid out of the car, and walked toward the house. He got out to follow her but stopped at the front-porch steps.

"I'm an idiot," he said. "Mo, I really am sorry."

As she opened the front door, she turned back to look at him.

"No big deal," she lied.

~ ~   ~

Ray woke early the next morning, furious with himself for being so careless. He wished he could undo the night before. He hated himself for hurting Mo, but it also scared him how much he liked the girl. She was someone he could see himself marrying in five or ten years. They would settle in their hometown, the place they both desperately loved, yet the place they both feared the most.

Mo, too, woke with the sun. She avoided thinking at all about the evening before. She felt antsy to get on the road, eager to leave behind all thoughts of home, to begin a new chapter filled with new possibilities. She dressed hurriedly and carried two of her packed suitcases down the stairs to start loading her father's sedan.

She set the bags down to open the back door. She saw something brown on the steps, thought at first it might be a dead animal. Denny's old glove lay there. How angry Billy must have been, how hurt and insignificant he must feel. She'd let him down with her lousy third-base coach's call, then failed to speak with him afterward. She should have apologized. She had been careless with Billy's feelings, too wrapped up in her own infatuation with Ray to tell the boy goodbye. She hoped she could make it up to him as soon as she got a chance.

Mo realized how stuck she had been since Denny's death. Like a desperate runner rounding third, unable to advance, yet unable to go back.

Home would never be the same. She knew that now. She would start a new life today. Leaving, starting college, promised new places, new ways to be. She would figure out where she belonged in the future.

She picked up her bags, stepped over the glove, and moved ahead.

Elaine Thomas

Elaine Thomas has published work in numerous journals and magazines, including *Syncopation Literary Journal* (which first published "Rounding Third"), *The Dead Mule School of Southern Literature, moonShine Review*, and *Pembroke Magazine*. She is a former winner of the North Carolina Writer's Network's Rose Post Creative Nonfiction Competition, and has been awarded several prizes in the Soul-Making Keats Literary Competition of the National League of American Pen Women. A retired college communications professional, she served as director of communications for Hampshire College (MA), Green Mountain College (VT), and her alma mater, St. Andrews College (NC). Thomas also holds an M.Div. from Duke Divinity School and is an on-call hospital chaplain. She lives in the beautiful coastal community of Wilmington, NC. She wrote "Rounding Third" shortly after news broke of the loss of Meat Loaf, one of her favorite rockers, and considers it a fictional tribute to his music and to small-town life in the southern United States.

Mouth Sewn Shut
By Mary Ellen Fox

Mother is hunched over the chest of drawers, her back bent so that her head has almost disappeared as she studies the white coffee rings on the old wooden surface. Her fingers work a skein of blue-tack back and forth, back and forth, kneading it into a gloopy mess. Martha's grey school pinafore dangles by one shoulder from the hanger hooked over the wardrobe door. It is a darkening afternoon in December. Martha hates this room.

'Did you write anything down Martha?'

'I dreamt I was naked, and Pauline Jackson was chasing me with a knitting needle.'

'Anything about Dolores?' Mother twists the skein of blue tack around her long white fingers.

'I don't really dream about Dolores. It's too.... difficult.'

'But there must be something Martha. Did you hear them speak? Where did they come from? You must have seen something.'

Martha sighs with irritation. How many times is Mother going to ask? She has told her over and over again that she only has the haziest recollection of events that took place two months ago and the most important details, such as the appearance of the men, have escaped her completely.

She recalls that it was an evening toward the end of Autumn, in the dead zone before the Christmas festivities kicked in. She remembered Halloween bunting listlessly stirring in the breeze outside one of the houses on the edge of Streatham Common. Her sister had picked her up from school that evening as their mother had taken a cleaning shift at the mental hospital. For some reason, known only to Dolores, they both walked back to their house along a deserted path through the rookery. Martha noticed that although autumn had stripped the trees, the roses were still in full bloom, glowing against the black of their foliage. She remembered the coarse cawing of the rooks roosting in the high branches and the woody fragrance of bonfire smoke and that two black shapes had moved behind the bushes.

She recalled scuffling and screaming. And she

remembered kneeling in a holly hedge and the prickles against her skin and the pain, sharp as iron brands, shooting up her arms, into her neck. And putting her fingers into her ears and singing to herself. Her teddy, Soft Mary, was there all the time pressed against her thigh. She must have knelt there for five minutes or more for when she looked up there was no sign of Dolores save for one black patent leather shoe. She wondered then why they had taken Dolores and not her. Martha counted on her fingers the possible reasons: Dolores was older by six years; Dolores had hair the color of beech trees in autumn, her own hair was blond and frizzy; Dolores had lots of friends, Martha only had Soft Mary; Dolores was tall and rangy whilst she was short and squat and rooted to the earth like a mushroom. Yes, that was definitely why: Dolores was thin and easy to carry whilst she was stuck to the ground and immoveable.

She was just mulling over the fact that the blood spots on the shoe shone brighter than the patent leather itself when suddenly all hell broke loose. People calling and torches flashing all over. Are you alright? Someone had called out. Martha looked up into the face of the local postman, Mr. Briars.

They took my sister. They took Dolores.

She noticed the swift shift of expression as Mr. Briars registered what she had said. Then more folk arrived. Martha heard them shouting Dolores's name. Somebody pulled her out of the bush and dragged her away. She dropped Soft Mary in the confusion. What was happening? Dolores was here and now gone. Teddy gone too.

And for some reason her mother wants to go over and over the incident again and again, almost on a daily basis now.

'I remember the bunting and it was really windy. And there were pumpkins outside the houses on Streatham Common North.'

'For Christ's sake Martha. You can remember every bloody detail on the pumpkins: the way the mouth was lop-sided and the seeds puking out of it. But you can't remember one single tiny thing about those.... those men.' Her voice cracked. An icy blade slid under Martha's heart. She wanted to stuff her fingers in her ears again.

'I've tried. I really have. I remember the puking pumpkin. It made me laugh.'

'Laugh? Jesus wept Martha. Do you know how I have suffered? Normal children would have remembered something or run for help or cried out. Your sister...'

Her sister what? The last words hung in the air like a swinging corpse. Her sister what? Had been smarter than her, prettier than her and of course braver than her. Yes, she knew all that.

'I told you to write something down in the notebook. As soon as you wake up write something down. You were the only witness, Martha. The only one that saw. You remember the nice policeman who came here last time? He said write something down, didn't he? So, write something. Anything.' Her fists come down on the drawer chest with such a force that a poster of Marc Bolan floats free from its moorings; the black kohl-rimmed eyes flash from under his mane of tight shiny curls. She stops at the door, does not look round but stretches up to her full height. 'There's another one here to speak to you. Another policeman.' And then with a tight throat. 'Please tell him all you know.'

Martha remembers the last policeman alright. And he wasn't that nice. He had long nose hairs and two blasts of broken veins on each cheek. This new one is much younger with reddish hair. He peers round the living room door and raps on it twice.

'Knock knock.' He says quietly

'Come in.' Martha believes this is the politest reply.

He takes off his helmet, ruffles his thinning thatch of strawberry blond and replaces the helmet again.

'May I ask you some more questions Miss Nicholls?' He speaks really softly and really slowly.

'You haven't asked me any yet.'

'So, Miss Nichols. What do you remember exactly?'

'Not much really.'

'You said there were two shadows in the bushes?'

'Yes, but I was counting the white roses, so I didn't see much'

'Were they tall shadows or short fat ones?'

'Well. The height of the shadows would depend on the angle of the moonlight.'

'Okay. Did you hear anything then when you saw the two shadows?'

'Only the rooks cawing. They were starting to roost.'

'You said you heard screaming?' The policeman's voice becomes higher in pitch.

'That was later. You asked me what I heard when I saw the shadows'

'Okay Miss Nicholls. Let's try something new. How did you feel about losing your sister?' His voice has a shrill tone to it.

'I feel like I have been cut open and stuff has been taken out and not put back properly and not in the right order.' The policeman's eyes widen.

'That is a very unusual description of grief.'

'It's how I feel.'

'Did you love her?'

'I don't really understand love but yes I guess so.'

'And yet you did not try to save her.'

'Well. I didn't know she had been taken until afterward. I wasn't really there'

'How is that? You were found in the holly bush.'

'Yes, but my mind goes elsewhere. When I am overwhelmed. I remove myself.'

'How convenient', the ginger policemen mutters

under his breath.

'It happens all the time. When I can't cope with stuff.' He licks the end of his pencil and writes something down in his notebook.

'Mother says everything's been shot to shit now Dolores has gone.'

'And you?' A ginger eyebrow arches.

'Me?'

'Yes Miss Nicholls. How do you feel?' He removes his helmet, ruffles his hair and puts it back on again.

'Oh. I just want her back.'

The sandy-haired policeman sighs like all the others. He decides that no new information is forthcoming, and he places his helmet back for the final time and shuffles toward the door. Martha feels that all too familiar mix of anger and confusion that accompanies so many of her exchanges. She did not see anything. That is the truth. Why does nobody understand? She had not really been there at all.

Mother and the policeman exchange words in the hallway. Martha watches as the policeman shakes his head in a dejected fashion whilst her mother looks down at her shoes.

Martha is constantly puzzled by Mother's behaviour. Only last night, Martha had been making her own supper. Beans and fish fingers. Her favourite. And she had been trying to open the can with the old tin opener which just left puncture marks round the edge and did not cut right through. Martha was just perusing on how her thoughts were very much like the beans swirling around in the tin, lots of ideas swimming around aimlessly in a thick goo rarely touching, never connecting and the rest of the world was similar to the tin opener jabbing away at the impenetrable tin trying to get to the beans inside.

With some effort a short slit had been gouged in the tin lid and Martha had tried pulling the lid free, urging it open with her index finger. Of course, one jagged metal edge had sliced it straight across and several beads of crimson had popped up immediately. Martha had not cried out at first, so relieved was she that the beans had finally been liberated. A few moments passed and the finger began to drip, and the pain was searing. So, she then let out the most piercing scream which went on for a

few minutes, way longer than it should have lasted. And
then Mother had rushed downstairs. Hearing the
commotion, she had stormed into the kitchen. Without a
word she dragged Martha to the sink and held the
bleeding hand under the gushing tap until the freezing
water numbed her finger. The same perfunctory ritual
was used to apply the plaster. All carried out in silence
apart from Martha's sobs which rose up from her
diaphragm with guttering breaths.

Life was always such a struggle and Martha always
assumed it was because she was a bad person. She had
always been plagued by the idea that her thoughts were
a little out of kilter and that she did not belong in this
world. She nearly always wanted to be on her own. She
liked walking home alone and playing with the dogs she
met along the way. She was always late for school. Her
mother could not even guess at the tornado of thoughts
swirling round her mind at any one time. She just could
never get into that can of beans. And how exhausting it
was every day to try and assemble those thoughts into
some meaningful chain. Mother had never hidden her
irritation for as long as Martha could remember. Why did

Martha not talk? She would ask this incessantly. Why did she have to nap during the day? Why did she disappear for hours? And where did she go? She was always interrogating her. But beautiful Dolores would always stick up for her little sis; 'Don't worry mum. She's just being Martha.' Martha was never sure what people wanted from her. So, she spent a lot of time guessing, pretending, panicking, trying to fit in. Not because she wanted to but because that was what was expected of her. Now it was just her and Mother. Tolerating each other. Being coolly civil because they had to share the same kitchen. Mother was right about one thing though: everything was shot to shit since Dolores passed.

In Martha's eyes she has come to see herself as more and more unlikeable. What had she done wrong? She ponders on this often when she is lying on her bed with Soft Mary. But the only thing she can come up with is that she is not Dolores. If only she could be more like her sister: look like her, act like her. Then everything would be okay again.

The room is just as Dolores left it. The bed still has the same sheets on it from the last time her sister slept there. There is a bottle of Oil of Olay, a lipstick, a black mascara stick with the lettering worn away, the beautiful revolving pendant with two halves of a broken heart, the Paddington bear that her boyfriend Phil gave her two Christmas ago and a couple of old Jackie magazines, all standing in a pool of dust on the dressing table.

She spies the box sticking out from under Dolores's bed. She pulls it out. It is a large hat box from some posh milliners, with a hinge. It is covered in delicate pastel flower decoupage and the name 'DOLORES' has been scrawled across it in Martha's own distinctive spidery hand. She opens it carefully. There is the ticket from the Wimbledon F.C. versus Celebrity Eleven football match that Dolores went to, a photo of Dolores and Martha at some Christmas party, a lock of her black hair in a little plastic jiffy bag that Martha had cut off whilst her sister was sleeping, some cheap rings that Martha found in the dressing table, one pink baby shoe from Clarkes with a little bear on it, a brown paper envelope with one of Dolores's school reports in it.

And there at the bottom sits the shoe, the black patent pump she took from the Rookery that grim

October. She went back the next morning to rescue Soft Mary and found the shoe under some leaves. It still has some specks of black mud on the heel and some rust-coloured patches inside the shoe and covering the toe. Martha's heart leaps although she has seen the shoe many times since then. She knows of course that the red-brown patches are not rust or mud but blood, Dolores's blood. She brought it home but hid it from her mother. Her own little private piece of Dolores. The police found the rest of Dolores's clothes, including her other shoe hanging from a bush in the white rose garden.

Martha plucks it from the box and gingerly places it on her palm and turns it round this way and that as though it is a priceless piece of Wedgewood. She looks at Marc Bolan to make sure he was not watching and then slowly she pokes her tongue out and licks the toe of the shoe until a tiny speck of the caked blood flakes off and rests on her tongue. She closes her eyes and sits there for a few minutes, with the afternoon sun on her face, until she can feel that the speck has dissolved, and the iron tang has all but disappeared.

She opens her eyes and stands in front of the long,

beveled mirror next to Dolores's bed. The room has been decorated like this for as long as Martha can remember. How many times had she watched Dolores's reflection turning in that mirror, smoothing an eyebrow, de-clogging her mascaraed eyes, pressing her full red mouth into a tissue?

A couple of evenings before the incident, Dolores offered to put make-up on her sister. Martha was hesitant at first, but her sister insisted.

'You could be so popular if you wanted to. If you just tried a little bit harder.' Dolores said as she carefully drew red lipstick round Martha's pale lips. 'You have loads of lovely blond hair. It just needs a bit of taming with some hairspray and there, look, bob's your uncle.' Dolores smoothed Martha's unruly locks with long white fingers.

'But I don't want to be popular. I just want to be left alone.'

'Okay li'l sis. Whatever you say.' Dolores saluted and then laughed her very Dolores-like laugh, head back and Adam's apple sliding up and down.

But Martha did not see what was funny. She never

did. It wasn't a joke, it was true. She was happiest alone. Sometimes she walked to school with Soft Mary on her shoulders. That was enough. She did not need people. People just confused her.

On the last full evening they spent together there was a heavy ring at the door which meant Phil had arrived. He was always on time to the minute. Dolores sprayed a cloud of Anais Anais into the air and twirled inside it on one tippy toe like the ballerina on the top of Martha's jewelry box.

'Gotta go sis. My chauffeur awaits.' She said, kissing Martha on the forehead.

Martha watched from the spare room window, as she always did, as Phil opened the passenger door of his gold Ford Cortina and Dolores, curtsying and laughing, slid her beautiful white legs across the vinyl seats. That was the last time she saw Phil until the funeral where he placed the Paddington bear atop Dolores's white coffin.

Martha turns to look into the mirror and lifts some strands up. The hairs are fair and coarse underneath and sometimes break away in her hand like spun glass. She carefully paints with the mascara wand from the roots to the tips until most of the lightness is covered in the gritty black paste. Satisfied that no fair hairs remain uncoated, she places the wand back in its tube. She props Soft Mary on the windowsill, as she often does these days, and asks her opinion.

'How do I look? Is my hair getting darker?'

But Soft Mary doesn't give anything away. Martha touches the end of her turned-up nose, "retroussé" Mother calls it. But Martha thinks it looks more like a snout. She stands next to the beveled edge of the mirror and moves the blue-tack marker up.

'Yep, I've definitely grown half an inch. What do you think Mary? Are my legs nearly as long as Dolores's?' But she knows they are stumpier than her sister's and with heavier ankles. Soft Mary just stares back with her one good bead of an eye, mouth sewn shut.

Martha carefully draws round her mouth with the red lipstick, turns her head this way and that to admire the effect and finally satisfied with the outcome, she pouts onto a tissue.

She looks out upon the garden. Late evening now. A plane, sharp as a needle, leaves a trail of white thread in the violet sky. An angry gust blows a layer of spent birch leaves upwards and they float gracefully earthward turning from yellow to gold.

Stung by her mother's coldness, she feels a blanket of weariness drop gently down on her like the sun falling, falling out of the sky. She wants to sleep and forget. And she has a belly ache; it came on when Dolores left her, and it has been with her ever since. She pulls Soft Mary toward her, tight into the knot in her stomach. Sometimes, the bear can make the pain go away for an hour or two. She removes her brown and orange tank-top and stretches out under the flowery cover. A flurry of images flutters behind her eyelids. Bunting stirring listlessly in an autumn breeze. A pumpkin with slits for eyes puking seeds onto the pavement. Air filled with smoke. And the jet black of the leaves of the roses in the white garden just like the strands of Dolores's hair blown horizontally across her pale face. She drifts for a second before the starless sky sucks her in.

Mary Ellen Fox

Mary was born in London to Irish immigrant parents. She graduated with a BSc honours degree in Chemical Engineering and obtained an accountancy qualification. After having her children, she gave up the glamourous world of accountancy and became a maths, chemistry and English language tutor. A creative writing course at City Lit in central London rekindled her passion for writing short stories and she has been short and long listed for many competitions and has had stories published in anthologies in UK, Ireland and USA. She currently resides in Epsom, home of the famous Derby horse race, with her husband, two children and a pair of hens named Tikka and Jalfrezi.

Jimmy's Swing
By Emely Bennett

The moving date I circled on my calendar so long ago had suddenly arrived and what a long, tiring day it's been. The rental moving van, parked in front of the house, had looked so huge when I first saw it pulling into the driveway this morning. I didn't think we would ever get it filled. Now it's finally loaded with the furniture I'm keeping and the boxes we've spent the past week packing so carefully. Memory boxes, I call them.

"There!" my son exclaims as he shuts the van's back door with a resounding bang. "The last box and we're finally finished! I don't know about the rest of you but I'm starving. Let's get cleaned up and get to that restaurant!"

Shouting one last goodbye, he and my granddaughters climb into his truck. Waving and calling my own goodbye from the front porch, I watch the truck make its way down the long, gravel driveway, followed closely behind by my grandson at the wheel of Jimmy's old pick-up. Smiling, I remember how Jimmy loved teaching our grandson the *"inner mysteries"* of that old truck. They had spent many happy hours together tinkering under its hood, which resulted in Jimmy and our grandson being the only two who could, **or would,** drive it.

Watching both vehicles disappear, I hear the sudden loud blast of the old pick-up's horn followed by peals of laughter. As both vehicles round the bend by the old maple tree, the distant echoes of horns and laughter fade away, becoming part of all the other early evening sounds.

That happy, boisterous group will soon be waiting for me and my daughter-in-law at the new restaurant in town. Having been too busy to stop for lunch, breaking only for the occasional coffee and muffin, we're all looking forward to the restaurant's special dinner buffet.

I decided to spend the night at the comfortable bed and breakfast not far from the restaurant and am meeting everyone at the new house tomorrow morning. The new house that, my family keeps assuring me, will feel like home in no time at all but, privately, I have my doubts.

I make my way to the back porch to wait for my daughter-in-law. She wanted to give each room one final check to make sure nothing had been left behind. She said it wouldn't take too long although I know she'll undoubtedly give each of the kitchen appliances one last polishing. Lowering myself into the old porch swing, it's hard to believe that tomorrow night I won't be sitting here, but I imagine the new owners will be – looking out over the garden as I am doing right now. Relaxing in the stillness of this warm June evening, I marvel at how fast the years have passed by. My thoughts drift back to the life that Jimmy and I shared here together. We had our ups and downs, of course, but we had lived simply, loving life, and cherishing each other and our family above all else. My last evening here – a perfect time for memories…

I am suddenly 18 again, working for the summer in the kitchen of the town's only diner. It was the usual busy Saturday morning as many of the locals met here every week for an early breakfast, catching up on the daily news and the neighbourly gossip of a small town. I overheard the regulars laughing together with Mick

Sullivan's nephew. He seemed to be well-liked by the
local farming community, but I found him very irritating
and I couldn't wait for him to leave. He had arrived from
Ireland three months earlier to help out on his uncle's
farm, planning to return home after the harvest. That
wasn't soon enough for me! Not a Saturday went by
when he didn't complain about the diner's breakfast
menu choices and, consequently, was never satisfied
with what he was served. His breakfast was either too
hot or too cold; too spicy or too bland – he seemed to
draw from a never-ending list of complaints. I couldn't
understand why he even bothered to come back every
week. That particular morning, after he had sent his
breakfast back yet again because the bacon was too
crispy and the scrambled eggs too soggy, I ran out of
patience. I took the plate from Jessie, the diner's longtime server, stormed out of the kitchen, marched to his
table, slammed his plate down, and told him exactly
what I thought he could do with his breakfast. He stood
up, gave me a crooked grin and told me he had only been
trying to get my attention and "praise be to all the Saints
in Ireland", it had finally worked! With everyone around

us laughing and obviously enjoying my embarrassment, I quickly headed back to the safety of the kitchen. He didn't return to Ireland but stayed here to take over the Sullivan farm when his uncle's health suddenly failed. Two years later, we were married.

Rocking slowly in the old swing, I hear its comforting creak as I look out at the garden. I remember the same quarrel Jimmy and I seemed to have every year but I had been so determined to have that garden! As one of those arguments floats by on the soft evening breeze, I smile, recalling that afternoon as if it were yesterday...

"I don't know why we have to go through this yet again, Jimmy. The yard back here could still use more colour. You know perfectly well you can't use this spot for anything else except to park that old tractor of yours and you can park that in the barn. Besides, it's not only flowers I'm going to plant and you know it. Have you forgotten the taste of those fresh vegetables we had last year? The tomatoes? The beans? The squash? The pumpkins? You couldn't seem to get enough of those pumpkin pies! Remember? And Jimmy, I thought we'd make the garden just a wee bit wider, plant more flower bulbs here, a couple of lilac bushes over there and I think that far border could definitely use something, too. Once that's all done, we should be able to see everything just fine from the back porch. Now, what do you think?"

"Just. A. Wee. Bit. Wider." Jimmy had slowly repeated each word as he reluctantly picked up his shovel. "You be saying the same thing, Girl, every spring for the past eight years! The way things are going," he continued to growl, "it be more flowers you be having back here than vegetables. We can't be eating flowers, can we now, and just why would we be needing to see them from the back porch?"

"Because it would be nice to have something to look at when we're sitting in our swing, Jimmy."

"And the sun's got to you, Girl! I be telling you what we be needing – seed and fertilizer for planting. Look at that barn door and it be hanging by one hinge. And over there – those old fence posts looking like they be falling down any day. It's surely not more flowers to look at from a swing we don't have that we be needing, is it now?"

"It would make me happy, Jimmy, if you would

build us a swing – you know, the kind we can sit in together, rock our baby, and enjoy the colours of our autumn flowers."

"First it be flowers, then a swing, and now a baby she be talking about," Jimmy had grumbled softly to himself.

I can still see his look of amazement as he suddenly realized that, after so many years, our miracle had finally happened. The shovel he had been working with so half-heartedly quickly dropped to the ground and, just as his arms had encircled me that long ago afternoon, the echoes of his whoops of joy encircle me now, easing the ever-present pain in my heart.

Resting my head back on the faded, worn cushion and, closing my eyes for a moment, I sigh and wonder how many times we had sat here together looking out over this garden. I can't remember the last time I had actually planted any vegetables, but I never lost that yearly argument. The flowers flourished, and every year covered the ground with a carpet of colour. I simply ignored his annual tirade, knowing that Jimmy had enjoyed that colourful display as much as I had. Another memory surfaces…

"Could you be coming out here a minute, Girl?" Jimmy had called from the back porch the day we brought our baby home from the hospital. As I stood speechless in the doorway, I could only stare.

"Well, don't just stand there, Girl, what do you make of it?"

There, on the back porch, hanging under the roof where two new beams had been added, was a beautiful, wooden swing, swaying gently in the morning breeze.

"Why, it's a swing, Jimmy!" I exclaimed as sudden tears slid down my cheeks. "But where did it come from? When did you do this?"

Shaking his head, Jimmy wrapped our baby son and me in one of his bear hugs.

"Spent half the night putting this up for you and the wee laddie. Now give over, Girl, and stop that crying. Never will understand why you always be crying when it's happy you're supposed to be," he said with that crooked grin on his face.

I tried to say something but there had been such a large lump in my throat, I couldn't speak.

"Oh, Jimmy." were the only words I was finally able

to whisper.

Despite what my son told me about low mortgage rates and investment opportunities, I will always believe it was Jimmy's swing and the garden that had captured the hearts of the new owners. The new owners – those words still sound so strange to me and I really must stop calling them that as they do have names. John and Rosie Murphy are a young, friendly couple with so many plans for their future. I like them, otherwise, I wouldn't have been able to part with the home Jimmy had worked so hard to provide for us, or the land he had tended so lovingly.

I smile once again as I remember the day they had come to view the farm. I had overheard Rosie talking to John. Seeing the garden for the first time, her voice had filled with excitement...

"John, look at that beautiful garden! Once the flowers are in bloom I know it will look just like a giant box of crayons that has toppled over. Can't you just see it? If we make it just a bit wider, we could even plant some vegetables. Can't you just taste them? John, look! There's even a swing on the back porch! We could sit there every night after dinner and talk about our day!"

"…and talk about our day," I whisper. Since the day he built the swing, Jimmy and I talked about everything right here. Should we plant wheat this year or beans? Should we put the new roof on the house now or wait until next year? Should we rent that extra pasture land from our neighbour? How can our son be old enough to drive when it seems only yesterday that Jimmy was holding him up on his first bicycle? He would be just fine, wouldn't he, at that university so far away?

It was here where we had found all our names haphazardly carved into the back of the swing by our eight-year-old boy. It was here where we had taken dozens of prom and graduation pictures. It was here where we met the girl our son would one day marry, and it was here where we had heard the exciting news that we were going to become grandparents.

On a quiet autumn night two years ago, with the smell of wood smoke in the air and the first star shining brightly in the night sky, it was here where Jimmy had gently sat me down, took my hand in his, and calmly told me what Dr. Jordan had explained to him that afternoon.

I miss him so much. Sitting here in the swing always seems to bring me comfort; I can almost feel him sitting next to me. The breeze is picking up, but the evening air is still warm and fragrant with the smell of lilacs. Lilacs. Jimmy continually complained about those lilacs...

"And if you had your way, Girl, you be having more lilacs growing on this farm than crops in the field," he always scolded.

He never fooled me, though. He always picked the season's first giant bouquet to be proudly displayed in the middle of our kitchen table. I didn't always get my way, of course, and there were many times over the years when Jimmy could be that same irritating Jimmy whom I had met so long ago at the diner. To be honest, though, I can be stubborn at times, although I'd rather refer to it as being "determined".

My heart aches knowing that I have no other choice but to leave our swing behind. I can always plant flowers and lilac bushes at the new house but what will I do without the comfort of Jimmy's swing? Earlier today, I had tried once again to explain this to my daughter-in-law and she had quickly replied, "Mother, I hope you know that all of us certainly understand how much this swing means to you. It means a lot to us, too, as we have our own memories sitting in it with both of you. The guys had a look at it and feel that trying to get it down would most likely cause damage to both the swing and the house. You know the Murphys want it so don't you think it's better to leave it right here where it's been hanging for all these years? If you must have a swing, I'm sure we can find one at that new lumber store in town. We'll take you there on the weekend so you can pick out the one you like, and we'll have them deliver it to your new house. I'm sure we can have them put it together and place it exactly where you want it. You do have a back porch at the new house which is very similar in size to this one so it shouldn't be a problem. Just think, you'll have a new swing without that irritating creak!"

I just couldn't seem to make this practical woman understand that I didn't want a new swing – it just wouldn't be the same. It's **this** swing, Jimmy's swing, that means so much to me, although I have to reluctantly admit that she is right. It does make more sense to leave

Jimmy's swing right here where it has always been. I'm sure the Murphys will give it the same loving care that we did and make their own memories sitting here together. Maybe at some future date, another eight-year-old child will haphazardly carve all their names into the back of it next to ours. I can't help but smile yet again, picturing that scene from the past. I knew Jimmy had secretly been proud of our son's carving efforts although he did give our son a very stern lecture about never taking a chisel without permission, followed by a detailed lesson on how to use it properly and safely.

The back door opens, and my daughter-in-law steps out onto the porch.

"I'm finished here, Mother," she says. "Are you ready to go? I don't want to rush you but we'll have to hurry if we're going to meet the others at the restaurant on time. We still have a few things to do at the new house tomorrow so the earlier we start the sooner we'll finish! Oh, don't forget to take that extra house key out from under that big red flowerpot to give to the Murphys. I'm just going to grab my purse and I'll meet you at your car."

"I'll be right there, dear, and thanks for reminding me about the key," I reply although I hadn't forgotten. I had already given it to my grandson earlier today. One of his friends is dropping him off here tomorrow morning to pick up the moving van, so he'll give it to the Murphys then. They're so excited to move in and planned to be here very early.

My daughter-in-law makes me smile. She loves to keep everyone and everything so organized. *"Time Management Personified"* is how our son lovingly describes her. Our son. He was so different from Jimmy and me and often filled us with wonder. When he turned 16, he told us what we had somehow always known. He loved the farm and respected our work, but it just wasn't in his heart to follow in our footsteps and work the land. He wasn't planning on giving up his farm roots entirely, though. Being around farm animals all his life, and helping Jimmy care for them, he wanted to pursue his dream and study for his veterinarian degree after graduating from the local high school.

"He doesn't have to be like us, does he now," Jimmy proudly told me later. "It's surely more than enough that he be of us."

I love our son and his family unconditionally but it's Me-Lad, as Jimmy had affectionately called our only grandson, who reminds me so much of my Jimmy.

"He does have a name, you know," I would often remind Jimmy.

"Don't we all, Girl, now don't we all," he always replied, with that crooked grin I loved so much.

Slowly getting up from Jimmy's swing, I take a final, heartfelt look at my garden, and gently caress the old, weathered wood for the last time.

"Goodbye, Jimmy," I whisper. "You promised that you'll always be watching over me, and I promised you that I'll move forward and live a happy life. I will try, but Jimmy I'm so sorry – I just don't know if I can keep my promise! I love and miss you so much!"

* * * * * * * * * * * * * *

It's morning, and walking into the new house, I can't help noticing the giant bouquet of lilacs sitting in the middle of the kitchen table. I wonder where they came from and I'm just about to ask when my grandson calls me from the back porch.

"Can you please come out here, Gran?"

"Of course, just give me a minute," I answer. "I want to smell these beautiful lilacs first."

As I stand speechless in the doorway to the back porch, I can only stare.

"Well, don't just stand there, Gran, what do you think?"

There, on the back porch, hanging under the roof where two new beams had been added, is a beautiful, old, weathered, wooden swing swaying gently in the morning breeze, accompanied by the sound of a familiar, comforting creak.

"Why, it's Jimmy's swing!" I exclaim as sudden tears slide down my cheeks. "But I don't understand – how did it get here? When did you do this? What are the Murphys going to say?"

"Dad and I spent half the night taking it down and the other half putting it back up here," my grandson answers with a familiar, crooked grin on his face.

"Now, give over and stop that crying, Gran. I'll just never understand why you always have to cry when you're supposed to be happy! And don't you worry about the Murphys. Once they heard the story of this swing, and how much it meant to you, both of them immediately insisted that it belonged with you, not them. John even spent last night putting up those new beams for us. He said to tell you that they already found a swing at that new lumber store in town, and they're picking it up tomorrow. Dad and I are going to help them put it together this weekend, and we'll place it in the same spot on the back porch where this one used to be. So, Gran, there's nothing for you to be fretting about!"

"The last time I saw Gramps," he adds softly, wrapping me in one of his bear hugs, "I told him to rest easy now and not be worrying. I'd always be around to do the watching over his Girl for him."

My eyes quickly fill with more tears as I look up into the sparkling blue ones of my grandson – the same brilliant blue that had been such a part of my life for over 50 years. He was the only one who shared that vibrant colour with my Jimmy.

I try to say something but there's such a large lump in my throat, I can't seem to speak.

"Oh, Jamie Me-Lad," are the only words I am finally

able to whisper.

Once my family's happy, noisy banter settles down a little, my son explains that, at first, they were planning on telling me. It was my grandson's idea to keep it a secret, and they had all immediately agreed, believing it would be a welcome surprise for me the first morning in my new house. My granddaughters admit that they almost told me yesterday when they saw how sad I looked believing that the swing had to be left behind. My daughter-in-law confesses how guilty she felt having to keep up such a charade every time I mentioned the subject of the swing. Sitting nonchalantly on the porch railing, my grandson just gives me another one of his crooked grins.

Laughing and giving everyone a big hug, I tell them that they'll never know how much their surprise means to me. After thanking them, I also congratulate them on their award-winning performances.

Basking in the realization that Jimmy's swing is actually here, I suddenly catch the quiet echo of Jimmy's laughter intermingling with the voices of my loved ones. As if pushed by unseen hands, Jimmy's swing seems to rock just a little faster in this morning's gentle breeze accompanied, as always, by its familiar, comforting creak.

I now understand that Jimmy will always be with me, wherever I am. He will forever have a cherished place with all of us - in our hearts, in our lives, and in our memories. He will always be remembered.

I am suddenly filled with a sense of peace. I am happy. I am home.

Emely Bennett

Growing up on a farm in southwestern Ontario, Emely spent many happy hours sitting beside her widowed grandmother on an old, leather loveseat in the glassed-in porch of her grandmother's house. She still recalls the comforting scent of lilacs and roses as they looked out over her grandmother's colourful flower garden and talked about their day; these particular memories would form the foundation of Jimmy's Swing. Emely moved away from the family farm when she was 18 but the memories of those special times shared with her grandmother remain with her to this very day.

Emely and her husband, Wayne, have three children (actually five counting their daughter-in-law and son-in-law) and eight grandchildren. After they retired, they sold their house near Toronto and purchased a farm in eastern Ontario and, after 50 years, returned to their country farm roots.

Being an avid reader ever since she was introduced to Dick, Jane, Sally, Spot and Puff in her Grade 1 reader, Emely can be found at any time of day with a book in her hand. In addition to her family, reading, gardening, volunteer work, and working on her next short story help keep Emely busy and out of trouble!

Rightful Magic
By Carol Campbell

I hold a small silver coin in my hand. I know it is silver because I bit into it. Silver tastes like tea that has steeped too long.

The man who gave me the coin is the husband and father of a family I served for fifteen years. I delivered to him four of his six children; the twins having arrived on their own before I could get there in time. But Master Bellows did not give me this coin as a form of payment. He gave it to me to find safe refuge when I fled the manor where I lived for forty years.

If I tried to use the coin in the town that I am approaching, it may be undervalued because it is so rare. Ancient, I was told, from the coast of Cyrene. One side is obscured, the face of Caesar is gone, worn down by the centuries spent perhaps in the pocket of a gentleman's coat or rubbed like a worry stone in a woman's cupped palm. The back of it, though, is better preserved, a clear engraving of a broadleaf plant. Could Master Bellows know that this plant furnished wealth to the nations who grew it before it was finally harvested to extinction? Could he know, as I had learned from the monk who taught me, it was once considered the most used birth control in the world? I recognized the plant. A plant called *Silphium*.

As hungry as I am and as cold as my hands are I have thought more than once about trading it for a cup of warm broth. I rub my hands briskly together, blowing stale warm breath across my knuckles. Looking up, I catch the scent of salt and rain before I emerge from the cover of trees.

I tuck the coin back into the soft layers between the hem and the second button of my frock and tie it shut with loose threads. I pat where it rests between my chest and my belly three times like a small drum. I have seen men tighten their belts and blow into their cupped hands as a superstitious practice as they march off to a battlefield for their lords. How we all create our own self-made charms to cope with fear.

I move my bag from one shoulder to the other. It is made of patchwork from remnants of different ladies' garments. Another habit I long ago adopted is to pet the soft velvet squares and the green satin diamond swatches but now they look sadly diminished, flattened dull patches. Inside are a few earthenware jars, clanking together, all corked tightly to hold the medicines I cannot bear to abandon.

I wish I had my winter cloak to travel with instead of this lighter one. It is wide but not thick. Parts of it are now felting. The blue-gray wool is not made for the cold and wet. It is meant for short distances, official visits, to new mothers when collecting payment after a safe delivery. Up until now I have had some protection from the thick wood. I pull it around me, a small comfort against the harsh breeze.

I reach the top of the cliffs, the edge of the world. The wind is full in my face and the bright sun makes me squint. The waves batter upon the rocks below. The soil is firm beneath my feet. I glimpse a town that sits along the sea. I've heard of this place, precariously situated between the cliffs and the water, a quaint village nestled within the rocks. Part of a building has lost its side wall to the surf, a crumbling cascade of pebbles and rocks stacked flat upon boulders besides high crashing waves. I think this town is called Hall Sands.

I descend the hill of rocky earth, holding my hands out slightly to keep my balance. The tall grasses grow with deep strong roots here, made stronger by the elements. I feel across the tops of the feathery strands, they are a different sort of plant than those I've seen.

There is a pier with boats, old wooden flatners mostly, used to collect fish from nets, crabs and prawns, I'm guessing. Muddy sliding vessels. Fishermen clean their traps and nets. People are going about their day near the water carrying baskets of oysters and fish, the gifts from the sea. They mill around the clusters of rocks and sand, their chatter rising to meet the sounds of waves crashing. The goat and sheep herders are behind me, wandering the small sandy pathways etched along the hillside. Women wear headdresses here, some have lappets, that move in the wind while they wring out their laundry within a small pool beyond the docks. I think about my own appearance. With my spittle, I wet the wiry curls at my temple tucking them with pins to the side of my head.

Near the dock, there is a small stone house with an open door and from it, I smell wafts of food cooking from a spit. I can only imagine what the source of the aromas must be: savory pies, roast hen. Stew from a day's worth of stewing. I am about to go to the house and beg for a morsel when I hear a scream coming from a child near the edge of the dock. My eyes, watering from the sharp whip of the breeze, turn to see several children running in circles on the hard-packed sand with their arms stretched out, like earthbound seagulls. One child, on the edge of the dock near the larger rocks, shrieks again, but it is with laughter as she is caught in her mother's arms. I remind myself that not every sound forevermore is an introduction to despair. The mother coos softly to her and after a while the child relents into the swell of her mother's embrace. I exhale in the realization I was holding my breath. The woman catches me watching and we both let out a little laugh at the impishness of children.

The woman confirms I am in Hall Sands. I thank her and she points to a tavern near the dock. I rewrap my cloak and turn toward the shelter, the wind instantly whipping my hood away from my forehead. I have no money to pay. Will they allow me to clean for a bowl of soup?

Before reaching the tavern by the docks, I pass a group of men crowded around a window of an old stone rowhouse sitting neatly along a cobbled path.

One of the elders of the group turns to me and nods as I grow closer. "Careful, Mother," he says. "This may upset you." I move to stand beside him. The western clouds, now strewn with pink and deep purple streaks, reflect on the greenish windowpane. It takes a moment to squint enough into the room to make a picture with my eyes. The candles inside the house are lit around three men who surround the body of a man. He lies face down on a table. They have begun a surgery on him.

I can't see the details except for a blurred rush of color. Pinks and grays near the back of the head. It appears the white tufts of hair from behind his ears have been peeled back. Inside, one man holds a candle while another sits and probes the area with a knife. Someone behind me moves quickly away and I hear vomiting a moment later. Others are as rapt as I am. I wish these eyes would not fail me yet. After a time, one of the men who is sitting in a chair closes the wound. We who are watching begin to move on.

"Nettie Dedham!" I am startled away from my thoughts. I look around. The voice that is calling still has no face. The figure comes closer. He may have been standing next to me a moment ago by the window.

It is a boy of twenty years or so. He is glad to see me, smiling as he is. As if he has found an agent of God. He has a limp. I can't tell if it's from birth or injury.

"Mother Dedham, what a surprise it is to see you."

He looks familiar. I may have delivered him. He can sense I don't know him. How does he recognize me?

"Dursome Caldwell, at your service. I remember you from long ago. I was just a boy when you helped my mother deliver the first of my sisters."

Ah, of course. That was a night made for stories. The mother was so close to death. It was more than just my efforts that saved her. Something else, the Blessed Ladies perhaps, the mother's own inner will. Or God.

"How did you know it was me?" At any other time, I would relish this encounter to hear of past patients and the lives they have led since my interference with the fates. But now I'm afraid that a wagging finger sits in wait around every corner. My name carries a dead weight.

Dursome tells me, "Your braid."

"How's that?"

"It is the same, long down your back. And your face is the same."

I marvel at such talents. Especially since I have been assured my looks are forgettable. We chat a bit about his mother who passed to God in the early months of last year. Sisters are both of age and healthy. Dursome says he is lonely for a wife and plans to travel on to a larger city, perhaps Somerset, to comb wool as many have started to do for a reliable coin. He leads me to a house and asks a woman with a long table for food. First, she offers a jug of ale and bread but then passes to Dursome a bowl of steaming rich and salty fish stew which warms my belly and limbs. The tingling in my fingers has lessened for the first time in days.

Dursome offers me a place to sleep, allowing me haystacks for a cot in the unused and weed-grown stables. There is no roof, but the low stone walls block some of the cold. I give him thanks and farewell telling him that I will be away by morning. He hands me a loaf of brown bread. I sniff at it, stale but edible. I stuff it into my bag. The haystacks are like piles of small sticks that poke and pinch at me when I sit upon them and several times yesterday I stepped into a muddy marsh which has kept my feet damp and toes partly numb. But I can smell the herbs through my bag and it lulls me somewhat. With my cloak as a blanket and my bag to rest my head upon, I find a broken sleep.

I awaken to a long-billed bird not an arm's length away. It's a curlew pecking around the top of the stable wall. Hard to see even in the brightest day: mottled-brown plumage makes for effective concealment from predators while they go about prying out worms and whatever else they do.

The bird stares at me for a moment and I her. Ah, she's looking at my bread, I realize. I take a bite and look up to see the heavens awakening, light reaching the many intervals of clouds and sky. The stars go quiet. I toss the curlew some crumbs. She stretches her wings at me and runs toward her breakfast. Then she is gone.

As I begin to head north, towards what I hope will be the town of Somerset, I think about my plight. I could change my name and be a nursemaid, since that is a position still suitable for mature women. But who would trust a stranger with their children? There is work to be found, I'm told, by the swell of sheep grazing in wide pastures from here to London. The wool combers are given food and a place to shelter, at least in some of the months. But I don't want any of these futures. I'm tired and my shoes are worn. Thinned from all the years of catching babes in the towns near home.

I hear someone calling my name. It is Dursome again. This time his shouts are pleas, full of anguished repetitions of, *Lord, where you be?* I instinctively grab my bag and go to meet him.

"Tis the ironsmith, Nettie Dedham. He's in so much pain. He needs doctoring." He must be speaking of the man who'd undergone surgery.

Dursome is crying when he reaches me. He smells like salt and he has brought me more food. A drumstick. Well, at least I think now it was his food but when he sees me staring, he hands it to me. I eat and listen.

"Please, Nurse Dedham, come help my ailing uncle. He's been in a bad way for a long time. The doctors have tried to help him, but now they've gone to York and won't you please come?"

This is foolish. I am not sure how much news about me has reached the area. But I follow Dursome nonetheless. This uncle, he says, began to have some kind of upsets of the mind and often times fell down appearing to sleep for long moments. Dursome tells me that the physicians were trying to employ a technique to make him better. But now the man has awoken and is in agony.

Water crashing on the rocks and the yell of the gulls cannot stop the wail of the ironsmith's cries from reaching my ears as we grow near. My stomach turns queasy. By all the saints, I don't even have a proper bag packed for this sort of work. I have a conversation with myself and realize that, most likely, all I'm doing is potentially easing the pain. Like I do for many of those who suffer into their passing.

I begin to ask questions as we hurry along. "Did the

physicians return to your uncle's residence?" No. "What exactly was the surgery?" Dursome shrugs his shoulders. His limp is more pronounced as he moves across the fields of damp and clay. Maybe it's worse in the mornings.

"But oh! One physician said they were trying to unite the wound that the injury caused."

"What by heaven does that mean?"

"I know not. But oh! They once said that he suffers from the malice of a bad humor because of a fall down the stairs. He slept for a long time when that happened."

I breathe deeply and we enter the stone house with windows that look out at the pier and the water. Morning has exposed all of the gruesome truths of the physicians' work. There is blood everywhere. A maid rushes in and out of the room trying her best to clean the floors, the chair, the sofa, the rugs. We go to another part of the house and find a woman sitting next to the bed where the patient lies. She is holding his hand which he allows for a minute and then shakes it off to grab at the cloth wrapped around his head. Blood is soaked through around the nape, where head and spine meet. The man's cries have become a constant moaning.

Dursome, for his part, is sad at the sight but looks to me and nods encouragingly. Then he says, introducing me to his aunt, "This is none other than the cunning woman of Odebury, Nettie Dedham. We are lucky to have her healing powers on this day. Pray, Aunt, will you let Nurse Dedham help us?"

The aunt nods. She is exhausted. Her wimple is wet from her tears and is splotched with brown spot stains that resemble food or blood. Up all night, praying, surely, she is trying not to think of life without her husband and provider. I would make her an infusion of valerian tea if I had my wares. She stands from the chair and bides me sit beside the man in bed. I gaze at him. He is gray.

I rummage through my bag and find at the bottom sleeping seeds, tiny round pills made of the essence of distilled herbs and flowers. They are so small I keep them in a special black pouch. This combination includes milk of the poppy, a plant that can only be found in Folkstone, a place of rocky crags and chalk white hills. I take out one of the pills and place it on the man's tongue who crunches it in his mouth. Even in his agonized state, the wretchedness of the taste causes him to wrinkle his nose and spit.

I reach forward and touch his arm. "Pray thee, wait a moment. It is medicine, a kind medicine to help you sleep and calm the spirit."

The woman comes back to the side of the bed and holds up a pewter cup to his lips. He takes two large swallows of ale and lies his head back down. She strokes his forehead. I absentmindedly stuff the pouch in one of my pockets. I move so she may sit beside him again.

"Will he live?" The woman says to me in her anguish.

"Madam, I know not. I am sorry."

She is crying ugly tears that fall against a puffy pink face. "Nurse, make him better!"

We sit together for a while. Dursome brings me a wooden cup and I drink. The ale is bitter but my tongue is less dry and swollen. I silently curse the men who were here only hours ago, who have moved on. Cunning women know to guard against the devil's trick of time's undoing. Where a patient might be fine one moment, they can easily slip beyond the door the next. And time can sometimes be a healer, true. Only watching and waiting will provide such answers. We sit together a while longer. Dursome and his aunt pray.

We both look to Dursome's uncle, Erik, he is called, who has stopped moaning and is gazing with a dull stare at his wife. The pain appears gone from his eyes. The sleeping seed is working. His shoulders relax. I reach into my bag again and feel for the tallest of my jars. I empty some herbs that will help to bind the incisions from the surgery into my hands and make a paste made wet with my spittle. I apply it gently under the bandage at the most exposed part of his wound. The ironsmith seems unaware of my actions. He gives his wife a look of reassurance. He squeezes her hand.

"All's well," he whispers. Then he sleeps, perhaps a final rest. We will not know until the morrow.

After a moment, though, the aunt grows alarmed, sitting up straight. "Is he sleeping?" I give a slow nod. The sleeping seeds can alter the timing of inhalations and the rhythm of the heart. He doesn't appear as though he is breathing.

The woman puts her hand under her husband's nose and tears up when she cannot find his breath. She looks at me as if I have brought a demon into her home. "Get out!!" She yells at me. I try to explain that these drugs have strange effects but then stand and go. Dursome hurries me to the front of the house and shuts the door behind me.

There is a boulder in my stomach, I am reminded that so much here reflects the peril of my own circumstances. The aunt showed no respect for me. Granted she was in her own emotional state. The fear of losing a loved one makes us all act in ways that we would not normally act. But there was something more in her glance. It was disdain.

I return to the hills behind the town and listen as the creatures speak to one another introducing the end of the day. The clouds are quick and move in animal shapes overhead. Closer to the horizon the slanted sunlight is gold against the birds' wings. There are tall legged storks fishing nearby. I am comforted by their presence.

When the last of daylight eases away from the woods and just as I have found an old worn path, I hear the whining of dogs. I know in my heart that they are searching for me. I am cursing at myself now.

Night claims the light from the alder and the beech. The covering of darkness does not give me hope that I will be undiscovered. As I feared, through the columns of trees I espy bright orange balls moving in and out of darkness – torches. The baying of dogs. I should just lie down and let them kill me but my heart is racing too fast to let me stop moving.

For all of my life, I have tried to help. And those who I have helped tend to be appreciative and discreet. But those in power, be it the state or church, have deemed my help a sin.

Last spring, I helped the lady of small manor procure a miscarriage. She was petrified to become pregnant again after the birth of her fifth child. That labor went on for four days. When she felt the tenderness in her breast and noted the absence of her monthly courses, I would not deny her the help. I gathered pennyroyal, cohosh, rue and mint. She drank the tea for two days and it worked. But we were found out by the chambermaid, a friend to the church who has since gone to study to become a midwife and a spy. When the constable began searching for me, I left home.

At the front of a group of large men is Dursome. He points his finger when he sees me as I, with my large cloak and heavy medicine bag, try to navigate down a hill into the thicker manse of woods. A dog jumps at my back and knocks me to the ground. I flail in the dead leaves, calling out more in fear than pain, my breath has left me. The beast pulls at my ankles with his bared teeth, biting, growling. A man calls him off. There are a few hoots as they lift me up, dragging me toward their village, only this time, I'm sure, there will no longer be the same courtesies from Dursome.

"Dursome, friend, what is this about?" Although, I already sense what he will say.

"Keep your tongue, old woman," one of the men shouts into my ear.

Dursome will not look at me now. He runs alone back to his own house. I am left with these men and they are rough. One takes my bag from me as we walk and I stumble. My skirts had been pulled down to my hips from the beast's attack and the men will not release my arms so I may correct my dress. I demand that they give me back my personal items, but one hits me with the edge of his wooden torch and I am silent from then on.

"Take her to the lock-up," a bearded man says. He, I learn, is the greave. I am sweating and shivering at once. They take me to a different area north of the Hall Sands village and put me in a chair inside a tiny house with no windows, just two bars across a small open space above the door for air to enter. The men depart, slamming the door shut with a clank. I call out, "What are my crimes?" but no one turns back to tell me. I watch them all fade into the night. Quiet engulfs the town.

On the night I left home, I went straight to a tavern run by a friend to ask for help. But I decided it was too risky to go inside and was about to steal a horse when Master Bellows found me. I had not seen him since the day he replaced me by a discreditable physician. I heard it said that Mistress Bellows had passed to God from childbed fever a few months ago under his care. I almost cried out when he touched my arm, but fell quiet because of the choked sob in his voice.

"My wife, my..." and then he bent forward, a broken

man. In the dark, I could only see the silhouette, though anyone can smell tears in the fragility of a painful moment. Finally, he cleared his throat and took a kerchief to blow his nose. "I owe you all apologies for my treatment of you these past few years. I didn't think, well." His demeanor is so different than that of the arrogant man who I had known as a neighbor and a well-to-do client for as many years as his daughters and sons had been alive.

He seemed to have forgotten what he wanted to say. Finally, he uttered softly, "I will make it right. We shall not mince words. You were a great comfort to my goodwife. I offer you this."

He handed me the coin. I couldn't tell the look of it. In the barn, the quiet was only disrupted by the horses nuzzling hay and by the swishing of their tails. I held tight to the silver piece. He went on, "If you show this to my cousin who lives in the western country near the shore, he will offer you housing, food, whatever you ask. He won't take the coin but is bound by its message. His name is Giles Allen and he runs an inn in Somerset. I will send word that you are coming. God be with you, Nettie

Dedham." He touched his fingers to his hat and mounted his horse. It was the kindest act any man had ever done for me.

In the small hut I sleep a fretful slumber while holding tight to my coin.

Dursome brings me lukewarm broth the next morning. There are a few thin slices of onion swimming at the bottom of the bowl and I do my best to savor the sweet crunch. But the food is gone in seconds. My head is pounding even though I found some sleep at last on the dry hard ground, cold as it was. As I set the bowl down, I ask, "Dursome, where is my bag?"

The boy shakes his head. "That shouldn't be what's in your thinking now, Nurse Dedham. They'll be wanting you for murder of the ironsmith." Dursome murmurs a prayer.

I knew this would be the case. God's nails, why did I follow him back in the first place?

"Who is my accuser?"

"The wife of he," and he looks away, ashamed. "My aunt."

"Dursome, find me my medicine bag and I will

depart from here. You will never see me again."

"They would whip me for that, and maybe worse."

"Will you fetch my bag?"

I study him. He's seriously considering. He knows I had no part in the death. But I have become the blame.

"What will you do with your bag? Will you make magic to harm others?"

"Dursome, hear me. I did not harm the ironsmith. I eased his pain."

"The greave said that he's been told only God can do that if the sufferer's earned the easement."

Yes, I understand this way of thinking. It's certainly true that my sleeping seed could have been what opened the door to his appointment with God. I weep in frustration. Dursome leaves.

A while later, the greave comes. "We have been discussing whether to call on the constable or the witchfinder to come for you." I put my head down. Several crows call out from the trees not far from me in the sway of a breeze on the branches beyond the town behind the hilly cliffs where my freedom is waiting for me. But the doors of my future close fast.

The greave starts to walk away. I dry my eyes on my now filthy sleeve and I say to him as clearly as I can, that I gave Erik the ironsmith something to ease his pain and that the surgery by the physicians was a deadly act. The greave turns back to face me and laughs dryly.

"This would be something a witch would say to distract folks from her true ill-bearing acts." He steps closer and says what I have feared all along, his pointy whiskers caught in his lips. "A witch by the name of Nettie Dedham was arrested in Oak Hill. Was to be taken to trial. There is talk that she escaped her captors to avoid being punished as God intended. That her magic carried her away to a distant region before she could be burned alive. I may believe such gossip. And there is a reward for her capture."

No one comes near me in this tiny house for the whole of the day. I am starving. There is nothing in my pockets but lavender crumbs. I eat them. I locate my tiny bag of sleeping seeds in my skirt pocket but leave them for now. I can decide what to do with them later if the worst of all possibilities proves true.

I hear children playing down the lane. I reach my

hand out and call to them in my sweetest voice. "Pray, Children," oh, but my voice is shrill and weak. "Bring a piece of bread, so hungry am I." This entices only jaunts from the unseen little ones and they throw rocks and clouds of dirt at my fingers. I wipe my hands and sit back down in my chair.

Dursome comes again in the hours before dawn. He brings me stale bread and water. The water tastes gritty but I drink it anyway and devour the food. He says he knows where my bag is. He has kept it for his aunt. I perk up. He says he feels responsible for the death of the ironsmith because he brought me here. After a moment he adds that he wants to help me because if they find out he brought a witch to town they will punish him severely.

He looks past me as he says, "They'll be asking you the questions and you won't be able to refuse the answering." I feel a little sick in my stomach. He leaves.

Sometime later the door jolts with a shutter and comes unlocked. A breeze pushes it open with little creaking noises. It is Dursome again, I'm thinking, the little mouse. I stand up from the corner where I had been dozing and am startled by the sight of the aunt who stands in the doorway.

"My husband is awake." She looks at me directly, gives me a tiny nod. Her wimple is gone. Her hair streams long and thick past her shoulders. Before she disappears into the dark, she says, "Cunning women are not valued as they once were." She hands me my bag. I clutch it to my chest, silent. The bag's contents clank together.

I run up the high sandy hills towards the line of trees. The earth is stirring. I can smell the raw pine and muddy bark that calls old memories to mind. Bended fern and short green shoots seek my attention as I gain speed, little promises of spring among the brown and decaying leaves. Where the thin tendrils of clouds meet the warm pink of sunrise it is as if heaven has come down upon the earth. I keep running.

Carol Campbell

A self-described *Jill of All Trades,* Carol raised two daughters and returned to school for a master's degree to focus on ending gender oppression. From award-winning theatrical and literary contributions to starting a new band with her husband, Carol decided that spending time doing everything she loves to do was the best tonic for empty nesting. She currently teaches Humanities courses at several Virginia community colleges and travels regionally as a lecturer, a musician and a dramaturg.

New Neighbors
By Karen Ekstrom

I'm an environmental consultant in Helena,
Montana, the state capitol and once—in the gold rush of
the late 1800s—the richest town per capita in the nation.
Those monied days are long gone, but many historical
buildings remain in a picturesque downtown. In April
1996, the population is just under 25,000 and the pace is
slow. I'm the lone rep of a large East-coast firm—a
biggish deal for a 30-something female in this industry
and time. We're expecting to grow, so, for now, my digs
are spacious—four rooms on the second floor of a granite
structure built in the heyday of the last century. I have
high ceilings and an ornate balcony with window boxes
that I fill with red geraniums in summer. So far, it's just
me and Dave, my three-year-old border collie, and, when
not busy writing reports or out making sales calls, I fling
a lime-green tennis ball and gaze out my diamond-paned
windows at Victorian architecture, tree-lined streets, and
imposing mountains that fade from purple to grey in the

distance. My western outpost is sometimes lonely but beats the hell out of a cubicle in a big-city, office park.

A 70s-era renovation of the building opened up walls and exposed hefty overhead joists. Blocking was added between the beams to cut down on noise transfer on each floor; but, like teeth, time has caused the foam chunks to loosen or fall out, and sounds from other offices sometimes filter in. I'm usually too busy to notice and, so far, no one has complained about the smack of the tennis ball and the occasional bark. We live and let live.

The office space beside me has recently acquired mysterious new tenants. Their door is unmarked, as is the signboard in the lobby. Even the suite number is missing as if the space had ceased to exist. Something else is curious. They've added a peephole and a deadbolt—the first I've seen in an office since I arrived in town a decade earlier. It's so unusual that I've taken to touching the tiny glass circle with the tip of my index finger as I pass. "Boop," I say softly as if tapping a baby's nose. Half the folks in town don't lock their doors, so this compulsion for security sets my imagination afire. I'm on the alert for voices in the hall, ready to spring out and rope these secretive neighbors into conversation. No luck so far.

Our shared wall is in what is basically a large closet that houses my copier and fax machine. As I wait for the unwieldy contraptions to warm up, I often hear muffled voices and catch the occasional word, but that's it. After a week of unbridled curiosity, I'm struck with a brilliant idea. I'll satisfy my need to know with a friendly visit to alert the mystery tenants to our shared sound and privacy issues. I'm puffed with pride at my overt show of neighborliness and my hidden guile.

Of course, their door is locked, so I knock and wait in the stuffy hall, hands behind my back as I scrutinize the threadbare carpet and wonder what to have for lunch. Fluorescent lights flicker and hum above me as the deadbolt clicks and a weathered face fills the narrow gap. "Yes?" the man says in a tone that drips with irritation. Hardly the greeting I expected.

Armed with my best sales-call grin, I look up to meet his eyes and sing out, "Hi, I'm your neighbor. I came to introduce myself. Can we chat?" My cheeks ache with forced joviality and my splayed hands suggest time spent in musical theater.

"Sorry. No." The door starts to close.

Undeterred, I press on. "It'll only take a minute." I lean in, expecting to be welcomed with apologies for his initial rudeness. Apologies that I'll accept graciously, knowing that we'll laugh about this incident in the future.

"You *can't* come in," he says, unmoved by my charm.

My smile dissolves in an instant. While this rudeness may be the norm in other parts of the country, in Montana it feels like a slap in the face. I poke my business card at his hairy fingers and hiss, "Fine! I'm trying to be nice, but you should know I hear *every* word you say over the wall between us." Shoulders back and chin up, I pivot and stalk the twenty paces to my office, sure he is watching. The whack of my door reverberates through the suite.

For several minutes, I pace from room to room and wallow in my inner child as Dave dogs my heels with his tennis ball seeking reassurance. "Who does he think he is, secret agent man? Of all the nerve!"

Eventually, I step out to the coolness of the exterior

balcony to breathe deeply and inspect my window boxes. It's too early to plant anything, so I weed out last year's remnants, wadding dry stems and leaves into a ball. The pleasure of my fingers burrowing in unfrozen soil and the sounds of crunching tires, quarreling magpies, and voices on the sidewalk below pull me from my funk and restore my mood.

Back at my desk, sun streams through the south-facing windows and I'm soon lost in crafting a report on smelter contamination. It's silent, but for the clack of the keyboard and Dave's soft snores. I stop to flex my fingers and sip coffee while Dave's paws twitch in pursuit of a Frisbee just beyond reach. My boorish neighbors are all but forgotten.

The door opens, and Dave and I look up as a dark-haired man steps in. Consultants don't get many drop-ins other than mail or parcel delivery, so I figure this guy is lost or fundraising. I swivel to face him and ask how I can help. He drops heavily into the seat across from me and then puts something on the desk between us. "We need to talk," he says with a face that looks like bad news.

A gold shield nestles in a worn, black-leather case. It looks real, although there are ways to get fake badges. Also, it's April 1st and a prank is not out of the question among my group of friends. Still, something in his face makes me believe him and I run a finger across the shiny surface, stalling for time. "What does the FBI want with me?" I ask in a measured tone, as beads of sweat build in my armpits and bra. I've nothing to hide but am the type of goody-two-shoes who gets heart palpitations at traffic stops. I've watched enough TV to know that the FBI doesn't pop in for a chat and cookies. This is serious. I've no desire to be on the receiving end of a strip search, to hear the snap of a latex glove as I bend forward, so I smile and do my best to look trustworthy while awaiting an answer, an answer that I know he is delaying in order to scrutinize my reaction. A lone droplet of perspiration trickles down my back and I squirm a bit but manage to stay silent.

Holding my gaze with unsettling steadiness, he says, "We're in the office next door. Your recent visit..." He pauses and I catch a hint of an eye roll. "It was, well... I need to know what you've heard." He scoops up his badge and puts it back in his pocket.

I grimace and release the ragged breath I didn't know I was holding. "Well, I was peeved at the reception I got when I stopped by, so I guess I exaggerated a tad." With a shrug, I explain the part about muffled voices, not whole sentences, especially when the copier is on. His posture softens, and he allows a tiny smile. After several minutes of what seems to be pointless small talk, he lets on that they're in the middle of a huge drug bust. My secrecy is vital. "Count on me," I assure him with a grin. "My lips are sealed." To my embarrassment, my fingers actually run an imaginary zipper across my mouth.

He leaves and returns with a ladder and the man I'd seen earlier, whose beetled glare now makes me look away as Dave growls softly. They inspect the copy room and confer in hushed tones, then disappear. Later, they return and stuff fiberglass batting into the gaps in the ceiling. I don't buy the drug bust ruse for a moment. It smells like a classic red herring, a misdirection. Why on earth would they spill the beans to me if the story were true? My mind whirls in search of something hot enough to bring the feds to town. Perhaps, they're surveilling the

"Freemen," a group of right-wing militia nuts bedeviling the agency in eastern Montana.

I'm not even close to being right.

Two days later, the news explodes. The FBI has captured their most-wanted fugitive, the Unabomber, putting an end to a seventeen-year reign of terror to protest the Industrial Revolution and the rise of technology. The only sighting of this mastermind had resulted in a sketch of a white man in a hoodie and aviator sunglasses. It's a sketch that I'm intimately familiar with as, a few months back, I'd rashly incorporated into a faux "wanted poster" that featured my former boss, Bob, as the "Una-Bobber." I'd faxed it to several former colleagues who were wildly amused until Bob himself lifted it out of the fax tray in the Denver office and went ballistic. Thankfully, in the 1990s, going viral was not a thing and the offending document now resided in my closed desk drawer. My artistic satire was inspired by the buzz surrounding the *Washington Post's* publication of the Unabomber's 35,000-word manifesto at the FBI's request. As hoped, the ramblings were recognized by someone who knew the author, who was acquainted with the unique style and tone. A brother stepped forward and contacted the agency to report what he feared was true.

After the arrest, the world learns how—from a one-room shack with no water or power in the deep, dark woods of Montana—the Unabomber crafted and wrapped bombs, then thumbed rides to Helena to catch a Greyhound to far-flung post offices, where he mailed his parcels of doom, hoping they'd do the maximum damage possible. Three people died and many were maimed by a Harvard-educated mathematician and former U.C. Berkeley professor, an anarchist who was completely under the radar in Montana, a state where a hermit in the woods is not worth mentioning, even one who looks eerily like Charles Manson on a bad day.

In the days that follow, the national and international media frenzy is intense as the pre-internet nation and world grapple for details. Kaczynski is washed and groomed and given an orange jumpsuit and a sport coat, transforming overnight from a grime-encrusted recluse to what looks like a middle-aged professional facing a DUI, albeit one wearing shackles and flanked by lawmen.

Alone in my office, I toss the tennis ball for Dave and wonder what ensued after I stalked off in a huff that morning. Was there panic behind the locked door about what the crazy lady knew? Local law enforcement had not yet been notified when I tossed my stink bomb of potential disclosure into their situation room. Agents could probably imagine me in the local coffee shop, blowing the whole operation sky high. "Large black, two creams. Did you hear the feds are in town to arrest the Unabomber?" What was the plan if the agent who was sent to see me decided that I knew too much after all? Would I be gagged and stuffed in a closet? Would the FBI silence me much the way my exasperated kindergarten teacher had done when she taped my mouth shut during a school performance so I would *"just shut up and play the damned triangle already."* I imploded their timeline for sure and can't help but wonder how often I've unwittingly caused chaos. Best not to know.

My testy neighbors stay a month or so, using the space to coordinate mop-up actions and compile paperwork. I hear snippets of conversation, which I pointedly ignore. Eventually, they decamp, and friendly new tenants move in who nod and smile the way folks are supposed to in a small town. I plant red geraniums in the window boxes, Ted Kaczynski is tried and goes to prison forever, and life in my sleepy little town moves on.

Karen Ekstrom

Karen Ekstrom is a geologist and environmental consultant based in Montana with stories to tell and an itch to put them on paper. After 40 years of writing technical tomes about waste site investigation and cleanup, she switched gears. It began with a newspaper column and evolved into novels and prize-winning short stories. In her spare time, she loves to hike, garden, and raft or kayak in her adopted home in the foothills of the Continental Divide. Her passion to write is supported by her husband and friends who will graciously read anything put before them. An obsessive border collie, two cats, and a flock of ungrateful hens keep her hopping.

Waiting Room
By Susan Evans

Lillis sits in the proctologist's waiting room, leafing through a magazine, trying to block out the mundane commentary coming from the tv. Henry, seated beside her, is "in" to have a biopsy. Lillis doesn't like waiting. She especially dislikes waiting rooms. This one is too large, and it's filled to the brim by too many old people, with their walkers and canes, their sniffles, and coughs. Why, they'll likely leave here in worse health than when they arrived.

Lillis doesn't ally Henry and herself with these waiting room patients, though in fact they are the selfsame in age if not appearance. Lillis takes pride in how vigorous and healthy she and Henry are for their age. Henry is tall and slender and still has most of his hair, which has only lately begun to show some grey, while Lillis is short and stocky with shapely legs and a hefty bust. Lillis is prone to take any occasion to report that she takes no medications, which seems to her a miracle for someone in her late sixties. And Henry's only health concern until now has been high cholesterol, which almost everyone seems to have, except herself, as Lillis is always quick to point out.

Henry is pretending to read a book. Lillis notes he hasn't turned a page in quite some time. She can tell he's nervous, though he says very little. Henry's the sort who will not ask her to come with him to an appointment for a biopsy.

"It's no big deal," Henry said when she suggested she accompany him. And then as an afterthought, "It's up to you."

"Are they putting you under? If they're putting you under, I'll need to drive you home."

Lillis could be bossy like this, which irritates Henry. But he is the type to ignore it rather than call her on it.

"Didn't say so," said Henry.

His usual loquacious self is what Lillis thinks. If it had been her on the phone, making the appointment, she would have asked. Henry never asks about anything. He just takes things as they come. Annoying as hell. So, she told him she was coming because she knows he really wants her there, even if he doesn't need her there.

The nurse calls for Henry, and he greets her with a smile and a cheerful comment as if he hasn't a care in the world. This is the thing that Lillis loves most about Henry. He's genetically pre-disposed to a positive attitude. But he turns to glance at Lillis just before stepping through the door, and she gives his raised eyebrow and questioning eyes a reassuring smile and nod. For a few minutes she tries but fails to fathom what it will be like to be sick and dying. That ending seems ultimately inevitable, but right now it seems far away when the sun is shining, the tv's blaring, and this is a day like any other. This will turn out to be nothing, is what she tells herself.

Lillis hears the ringtone and buzz of her cell phone, muffled deep in the recesses of her purse, but loud enough to cause a small stir among the waiting-room patients seated nearby. It takes her a minute to locate the phone and by the time she does, the caller has hung up. So annoying, thinks Lillis.

She sees the call was from her daughter, Lizzie, which surprises her. Lizzie rarely phones. Invariably their phone conversations are initiated by Lillis. Maybe she was calling to ask about the biopsy, thinks Lillis, trying to remember if they had discussed the procedure during their most recent conversation.

Calls with Lizzie are always short. What is there to say? To Lillis, her oldest child seems like a person from her past she hardly knows anymore. She has a hard time reconciling her forty-year-old daughter with the chatty toddler who held Lillis' hand while tucked into her car seat on the way to daycare, or the sweet child Lillis pushed on the backyard swing, back and forth, back and forth, Lizzie's long blond hair billowing out behind her and her skinny legs straight as sticks out in front of her. Lizzie's teen years had been less sweet, thought Lillis, but that was to be expected. When Lizzie moved on to a college, several hours away from home, Lillis thought it was ideal. She didn't want her daughter returning every weekend. And Lizzie hadn't. Henry and Lillis had experienced a bit of empty nest syndrome, but at the time they still had Michael at home. Then, after graduation, Lizzie moved to the opposite side of the country and never returned.

Each year that passed it seemed Lizzie grew more distant. After all this time, Henry and Lillis were no longer part of her life in any significant way. Lizzie hadn't been back home for a visit in the last six years. If they wanted to see her in person, Lillis and Henry must travel to her.

Their last trip west to see her had been a disappointment. The occasion was Lizzie's birthday and Lillis had suggested she and Henry visit for the celebration. In truth, neither Lillis nor Henry felt very celebratory about this occasion. At almost middle age, their daughter remained unmarried and seemed uninterested in starting a family. Instead, Lizzie had a 'big job' (as Lillis described it to her friends) in the movie industry. Though Lillis was always pleased to tout Lizzie's career accomplishments, both Lillis and Henry could see the writing on the wall...there would be no family, no children in their daughter's future.

This birthday was Lizzie's big four-oh and she had planned a very fancy party to be held at her very fancy home in West LA. Because of all the doings, she arranged for Lillis and Henry to stay at a nearby hotel during their visit. Lillis had been miffed.

"What are we? Long distance relatives?" Lillis asked Henry as they were settling into their hotel room.

Henry didn't bother to point out that in fact they were.

"I think she has four bedrooms in that house of hers," said Lillis.

Henry had not engaged with Lillis, which miffed her further. She would have liked a little back-up support. But Henry merely stood at the window and said, "It's a nice view of the city, Lil. Come have a look."

And Lillis had grudgingly looked.

Lillis and Henry understood that their daughter was busy with details the following day as she prepared for the party that was to be later that evening. Lizzie had provided them with an itinerary for the day that did not include a need for their help at her house. She pointed out that her professional party planner employed a decorator, a caterer, a bartender, even parking attendants for the party. And the house was tidy, elegant, and party-ready as always. (Who was home all day to make a mess? No one, that's who, thought Lillis.)

After spending the day pretending to be tourists, Lillis and Henry dressed for the party and were whisked to Lizzie's house in the car that was arranged for them. Henry estimated there were at least sixty party attendees. He and Lillis spent the good part of an hour making the rounds of the various rooms so he could calculate his estimation. They chatted for a while with Lizzie's executive assistant who Lillis suspected had been assigned to keep an eye on the two of them. The worst part of the evening had been when Lizzie introduced them to her latest live-in boyfriend. She didn't call him that, but Lillis got the picture and clued in Henry.

The basic facts were that his name was Leroy; by night he played bass in a band of no renown and by day worked as a film editor on a streaming tv show that neither Lillis nor Henry had ever heard of. He seemed friendly enough, and Lillis could get past the ponytail hair style and the tattoos on his neck and arms. The main problem was that he appeared to be quite a lot younger than Lizzie. Later they learned he was only twenty-eight. Lillis felt embarrassed for her daughter. It just seemed to Lillis to be a bad idea. When Lizzie mentioned the age difference, Henry couldn't look her in the eye, while Lillis raised her eyebrows and delivered a look of disapproval. But neither of them said a thing. It wasn't their place. They didn't like to interfere.

The day after the party, Lizzie called to say it was a busy time of the year for her at the office and she couldn't take time off during the next couple of days. She would be able to meet them later at a restaurant for a nice dinner. Lillis and Henry had seen enough of the LA tourist sites by then, so they paid the ridiculously high change fees and flew home early.

The biopsy procedure doesn't take long and afterwards, Lillis and Henry head home where he spends the afternoon on the sofa watching television. She makes him cocoa and toast, then spends the remainder of the day in the yard, blowing the fall leaves into the street, and trimming back the Japanese Anemones. Gardening has always been an enthusiasm of Lillis', but since retirement, it is her purpose for getting out of bed in the morning.

Lillis' garden is most lush and lovely in Spring,

spilling over with all manner of perennials, flowering bushes, and climbing vines. Bluestone paths and steppingstones wind through the yard, ending at the wisteria-topped arbor in the back by the fence. But today it's late fall, and her garden is dying back for winter. The coneflowers have been picked clean by the finches; the daylilies are still mostly green, but floppy, their flowers done for the season; the clematis have dropped their leaves, leaving their tangled brown, flowerless vines on their trellises to winter over for next spring's flowers, and all the creamy white wind flowers are gone from the Japanese anemones – only the tall, flowerless stems wave with the chilly wind. While the winter garden isn't Lillis' favorite, she appreciates the quiet peacefulness of the garden in this season. There's much to do to prepare the beds for next year's bloom and she loses herself in the rhythmic work of trimming, raking, digging, and pulling. It's nearly dark when she finishes.

She's removing her rubber garden shoes and gloves in the back hallway when she hears the murmur of voices coming from the living room. Lillis heads in that direction and recognizes Michael's voice and then his laugh, and this causes her to suddenly remember that it is Wednesday.

"Michael, we completely forgot what day it is," she says as she greets her son with a brief hug.

"I told him, Lil," says Henry. "It was that damn doctor's appointment today. Threw us off our schedule," he directs this last to Michael.

The three of them have a standing dinner engagement at six o'clock on Wednesdays.

"I'm here now." says Michael. He's a handsome man, like his father, but closer in height to Lillis. "You haven't eaten yet, right? Dad are you good to go out?"

"Hells bells," says Henry, "I'm as good as I ever am, and hungry too."

Michael drives. Henry sits up front while Lillis is squeezed into the back of Michael's sporty SUV. The restaurant destination is their longtime favorite Italian eatery, where they take a booth in the back, each ordering the exact same meal they had on their previous visit...pizza for Michael, carbonara for Henry, and ravioli for Lillis. Lillis is the only one of the three who sometimes varies her order. The others tend to stick with their favorites. And Lillis is the only one who orders a cocktail...Manhattan rocks is her usual.

Their weekly dinner routine is a tradition Lillis instituted the previous year when Michael's wife of fifteen years left him, taking their two children to live two hours away upstate. Lillis and Henry were shocked and devastated at this development. They were particularly fond of Michael's wife Charlene and, of course, their grandchildren. It seemed impossible that this could have happened.

Lillis remembers the last time they all were together... the occasion was Henry's retirement dinner. Michael, Charlene, and the children all attended together. It was like every other family gathering for the past fifteen years. There was never a hint of any problem. And then wham! Less than a week later, Michael phoned to say that he and Charlene were splitting up, and Michael was moving into an apartment. Within six months, Charlene up and moved to the town where her sister lives, a two-hour drive away from Michael and Lillis and Henry.

Agreeable, attractive, and generous Charlene...Lillis

and Henry thought of her as their own daughter. And
Lillis often remarked what a wonderful mother Charlene
was ... so kind and patient with the children.

"What the hell happened?" Henry asked Lillis when
they learned the news.

"You're asking me?" replied Lillis.

They were both dumbfounded. Michael provided
little in the way of explanation other than to say that
Charlene had cuckolded him. Lillis had to look that word
up in the dictionary.

"I think he means Charlene had an affair," Lillis
explained to Henry.

"I don't believe it," said Henry. "Charlene is not the
type."

Lillis just shook her head. It was true that Charlene
didn't seem the type. But in most things, Lillis is
generally less idealistic than Henry. She could see that it
could have happened. Michael wasn't the easiest person
to get along with. He was her son, but she knew that he
could be a little self-centered and a bit of a pompous ass
at times. She couldn't help thinking there was more to it
than he was saying.

Charlene had written them a letter, which Lillis kept in the bottom of her jewelry box. It said how sorry she was and how much she loved both Lillis and Henry and that she hoped they would be able to keep the lines of communication open. Lillis mentioned the letter to Michael, thinking perhaps it meant Charlene wanted to work things out. But instead of helping the situation, Michael blew up at Lillis and said, "You always liked Charlene more than me!" And then he said that as their son, he deserved their support, and it was either her (Charlene) or him (Michael) in Lillis and Henry's life. Well, that put the kibosh on any further communication with Charlene.

They held out hope that perhaps the whole thing would blow over after a time. Lillis had tried (going against her policy of not interfering in her children's affairs) to talk sense into Michael. But she remembered that he had been a stubborn child who was now a stubborn and inflexible adult. It broke Lillis' heart that he seemed unable to grasp what he was giving up.

The lines of communication between Lillis and Henry and Charlene remained closed. Lillis had sent

Charlene a Christmas card. They saw the children when Michael drove the two hours north to bring them down for a week or weekend here and there. At the end of these visits Lillis always asked after their mother and told them to tell Charlene hello from Lillis and Henry. They continued to mourn their loss of Charlene. This, of course, they kept to themselves. It wouldn't have helped matters to let Michael know of their sorrow.

"So, Lizzie called me today," Michael announces as they are finishing their entrees.

"In the middle of the day?" asks Lillis. She spills a little of her drink when she sets it down too quickly on the table.

"Yeah, a real surprise," says Michael, who typically speaks by phone with his sister only on major holidays. He's placing the remainder of his pizza into a to-go box. Michael always orders the pizza so he can take half home for dinner the next day. He's a bit of a penny-pincher.

"What did our Lizzie have to say?" Henry asks. Lillis notes that he says this in a cheerful, naïve manner as if Lizzie phones like this all the time.

"She called me today too," says Lillis, just now

remembering. "I forgot to call her back. She didn't leave a message."

"She thinks we should talk to you two about moving," says Michael. He doesn't look either Lillis or Henry in the eye as he says this and seems to be taking a very long time to move his pizza into the to-go box.

"Moving? Why the hell would we move?" demands Henry. He has stopped eating, his fork halfway to his mouth. He gives Lillis a questioning look as if to ask her if she knows something about this.

"We have no intention of moving," says Lillis definitively. Topic closed.

"It was Lizzie's idea, not mine," says Michael. "She thinks you should move into one of those senior living places. No stairs, emergency help. That sort of thing. She'll probably call you about it again. She seemed pretty sold on the idea." Michael's attitude is that he is merely delivering the message but has no real opinion on the matter.

Lillis shakes her head in disgust. "What does Lizzie know about what we need. She hasn't been here to see us in almost a decade." She gulps down the remainder of her Manhattan and considers ordering another one. This is so Lizzie. Thinks she's in charge of the world. Lillis remembers when Lizzie was heading off to college – Lillis' greatest desire was for Lizzie to become a successful, independent career woman. She wonders if it is her own fault that now Lizzie has gone too far in that direction. How could she have known that encouraging her daughter to follow her dreams would ultimately lead to this distance, this estrangement? Lillis does not understand it.

"I bet Lizzie could get you into a pretty nice place if you wanted. You know she can afford it," says Michael. He seems oblivious to Henry's befuddlement and Lillis' fury.

"We already have a pretty nice place, and we didn't need Lizzie's help to get it," says Lillis.

"I'm just saying that I'd take her up on it if she offered to buy me a nice place," says Michael.

"Anything happens to me, you'll look after your mother," Henry interjects. "She wants to stay where she is. She has her garden and her friends there."

"What are you talking about Henry?I don't need

anyone to look after me."

"I'm just saying that someday you might need Michael's help. If I'm not here. That's all," he has laid down his fork and stopped eating.

"Well, you're not going anywhere so it's a moot point," says Lillis. She notices Michael's silence on the matter. How much help would he be, anyway, is what Lillis thinks. He is not at all useful around the house the way Henry is.

Lillis has begun to work her way out of the booth. "Come on Henry. I'm ready to go home."

Henry starts to push back from the table, as Michael says, "Hold on Mom. We don't have the check yet."

"Why don't you get it dear," says Lillis. "Your Dad and I will meet you outside."

"Oh," says Michael, briefly confused. "Well, I thought you were treating tonight."

"Well maybe just this once you could take care of it," says Lillis, her annoyance clear as she marches to the front of the restaurant, leaving Henry and Michael to sort it out.

Lillis and Henry are bundled up against the chilly air for their evening walk. Both are wearing their heavier jackets and knit hats pulled down over their ears. They take it slow, in deference to the doctor's orders that Henry not overexert. Lillis' hand is in the pocket of Henry's jacket because that is the way they always walk together. In synch, arms linked, her hand held within his, enclosed in his jacket pocket.

They're quiet as they walk. Lillis is still thinking about her children, but the flare of her temper from earlier has faded. She says, "How did this happen, Henry? I don't think our children like us anymore. And sometimes I don't think I like them that much either."

"Now Lil, you don't mean that."

"Which part?" asks Lillis.

"They have their own lives is all, Lil," says Henry.

"Not the lives I thought they'd have," she says. Not the lives I wanted them to have, is what she thinks. Lillis wonders if this is because she didn't expect enough of her children when they were younger. Or if the problem is now her expectations are too high. As she is sometimes prone to do, she despairs that although she knows she tried to be a good mother to them, she fears she was not good enough.

In reply, Henry squeezes her hand.

She envies that Henry does not feel responsible for their children's failures and futures the way that she does. She has never been able to let go the feeling that she should be able to fix things, to arrange things, as she did when they were young.

She says, "It makes you think about your life doesn't it, Henry? The choices we've made. Suddenly it feels like time is short."

Henry nods his head. "It does, Lil. It does."

Their evening walk takes them through neighboring streets where the residences are a mix of moderately sized bungalows and ranchers with tidy, landscaped front yards. Both Lillis and Henry enjoy walking past these homes at night, glimpsing the lives of those within through their lighted front windows. All is quiet along their way, an occasional jogger or dog walker passing them by.

Henry seems especially subdued, and Lillis wonders if he is thinking about the biopsy. If it turns out to be something, they will get a second opinion, is what Lillis thinks. A well-respected teaching hospital is within a two-hour drive, and they will go there for treatment if needed. She will talk Henry into chemo if it is advised. He has said in the past that he would never do chemo, but she is certain she can convince him. They will do whatever it takes, Lillis decides.

She says, "Henry, I don't think we should worry until we hear back from the doctor with the biopsy results. It will probably turn out to be nothing."

Henry says. "It is what it is."

Lillis is quiet for a few moments, and then in a wistful voice says, "I just don't want anything to change." She doesn't expect a reply. She's simply voicing what she knows they both are feeling.

Henry doesn't answer, and so she looks up at him. It's hard to discern his features in the dark, but at that moment they are near a streetlamp and Lillis believes she can see tears on the edges of his eyes. She gives Henry's hand a squeeze. She doesn't mention the tears because that would embarrass Henry to no end.

It's fully dark outside now, so chilly for an autumn

night. Henry stops on the sidewalk and pulls Lillis to him in an embrace. She lingers there, her head on Henry's chest, his arms tight around her, pressing his warmth into her. Over his shoulder, she sees a sprinkling of stars shimmer in the night sky.

Susan Evans

Susan Evans is a recently retired entrepreneur, having founded two educational technology companies, where she served as CEO for nineteen years. An avid reader, her recent retirement has afforded the opportunity to return to an early interest in fiction writing. Her undergraduate degree from Indiana State University included a minor in Creative Writing and a double major in Journalism and Psychology. She also holds a Masters in Research Psychology. She resides in Richmond, Virginia.

The Blessings of Grasshoppers
By Adele Evershed

I watch you sleep as I used to when we first brought you home from the hospital. The old feelings of dread and wonder are back and lodged in my stomach; they fill me up, so I forget that I need to eat. It was so easy those first few months; your mother's breast milk was all you needed--all the vitamins, proteins, and fat. And best of all it was always available, the perfect fast food. I was astonished to discover you didn't even need water. Your mother spent hours pouring over websites that explained the best position for breastfeeding or how to overcome the problems of sore nipples. Her own mother was no help. She had fed her own babies powdered milk. Your grandmother told your Mom a nurse had said that her breast milk would be too thin to keep a baby well-fed and gave her some free formula in a ready-to-feed bottle.

As you got older, we felt so lucky that you were never a picky eater; unlike some children, we knew your cousin, Ben, would only eat cereal and French fries.

Finally, it got so bad that your aunt had to take him to a nutritional psychologist. I remember laughing when she told me that according to the doctor, a child could learn to eat, but they can also be taught not to eat by the circumstances of their lives. I jokily said, "That explains everything then. Poor Ben has learned not to eat because of your awful cooking." I think about that conversation a lot.

You smile in your sleep, your eyelids rippling, and I wonder what you might be dreaming. Maybe you're remembering catching your first fish. My voice had woken you up like an alarm. I had been arguing with your grandfather, he insisted girls didn't need to know how to fish, so my voice was high-pitched when I called your name. We ran into the day to collect grasshoppers in the long grass, whacking them with your bright birthday cap. Later you rested your tongue on your lower lip and drew your brows down as you ran the hook through the chattering body. We stood on the bank of the lake as the insects dabbled on the surface of the water under the lazy setting sun, listening as they shook a musical retreat from their bodies. You held the reel at your waist as you picked out a target in the water. I bit my tongue so hard to stop myself from giving you a running commentary, and the rusty flavor of blood flooded my mouth. It felt fitting, a coming-of-age ritual that tasted as old as the dance of the seen-it-all-before bog turtles. You sent the line soaring, a whipping lunar arc over the deeper water, tearing the sky in half. Almost as soon as the grasshopper hit the surface, a crappie was on the end of your hook. It was the perfect skillet size. Its mottled skin shimmered in the mellow, fleeing sun; we both whooped loud enough to raise the childishly colored bunting birds that rose in sugary sprinkles against the pink sky. Was that our last perfect day?

Heading home, you were flushed and animated with your success. We both watched your grandfather as he took his filleting knife and pushed his sleeves up as if he were a surgeon about to perform a delicate operation. He hummed like the cicadas as he cut behind the gills. We both knew better than to say anything as he offered up his wordless elegy for the bounty of nature. He ran the knife smoothly along the backbone and gently pulled meat from the ribcage. Finally, taking care not to rip it, he ran his knife along the thin skin. He placed the fillets into a bowl of salt water and put them in the fridge. Then, he ruffled your hair and said, "Well done, young 'un. I didn't catch my first fish 'til I was nine". You asked to eat the crappie for supper. But my father shook his head and told you, "Fillets need soaking overnight to keep the meat nice and tender fur cooking; we've grits and collard greens fur tonight." You were impatient to taste what you had worked so hard to catch and started to argue, but your grandfather would have none of it. He rubbed a hand over his waffle cheeks and said, "Listen, Kitten, your Daddy and I disagree about how long an egg should be boiled fur, but we both know some things in life cannot be forced onto our timetable. We'll eat your fish tomorrow. Now go wash up. You're making more commotion than I have sanity fur." You did roll your eyes and snapped, "My name's Kit, not Kitten," but you went to the sink.

Later as I was coming to say goodnight, I heard your voice talking excitedly even though I knew you were alone. Eavesdropping at the door, my heart felt heavy as I realized you were telling your mother all about your day. Like every good fisherman, you had inflated the size of the crappie; it would now be capable of feeding a small village. And then you said, "Momma can you tell Jesus what a good fisherman I am? I'm going to catch lots and lots of fish. Goodnight, Momma, love you." When I stuck my head around the door, you said, "Daddy, I've decided what I want fur Christmas. I'm going to ask Santa fur a knife." I smiled and corrected you, "It's 'for' like the number, not 'fur' like the skin of a bear." You pulled your lips into a tight line and replied, "But Gramps says fur, and you never correct him."

It was an old argument that I refused to get drawn into again just to delay bedtime, so instead, I told you that you were too young for a knife and why not ask for an American Girl doll instead. You shook your head so fiercely your hair whipped into your eyes, making them tear up as you pleaded, "No, Daddy, I want a knife FOR filleting my own fish. I watched Gramps, so I know I can do it. I just need a knife." I stroked your hair behind your ears and shushed you.

The next day I let you measure the cornmeal, flour, cayenne pepper, and Tony Chachere's Creole seasoning mix into the plastic bowl. After putting the lid on, I told you, "Shake it like you're ringing the bells of heaven for the return of another lost soul." It was something my mother, your Grammy, always said to me when she let me help in her kitchen. You giggled and gave the expected response, "Halleluiah." Then, I supervised as you dipped the damp fillets into the coating, "Put one in at a time, or you'll get the meal wet, and then it won't stick."

Your grandfather shuffled into the kitchen, lured by the smell of the hot oil just as I was about to drop a couple of coated fish into the pan and said, "Put one in at a time, or you'll cool the oil, and then they won't crisp up." I sucked my teeth in irritation, not recognizing the echo of his words in my own two minutes earlier. He hovered over my shoulder, telling me when to flip the fish, so I felt my smile escape into the steam. As I scooped the golden-brown fillets onto a paper towel, my father asked what I had done with the fish bones. When I told him, he sighed and said, "Jakey, I thought I'd taught you better than that! We could've fried 'em up, waste not want not." I blotted my good mood on the paper towel with the oil from the fish and tipped them roughly onto three plates. As I carried them into the dining room, I saw you had laid the table with your mother's silver that we only brought out at Christmas. Seeing my face, you bit your lip and said, "That's okay, isn't it, Daddy? I wanted Momma to be part of the meal, but I can go get the knives and forks from the kitchen drawer if you want me to?" I turned back to the kitchen to blink away my tears and rescue my smile, nodding that, of course, it was more than all right.

A southern fish fry used to be as ubiquitous as beavers in South Carolina, but that meal was unique, and the memory has lasted longer than any fossilized beaver dam ever could. The creole seasoning fizzed, the batter crunched satisfyingly, and the crappie tasted soft and subtle. In between bites, you told your grandfather how you wanted a knife for Christmas so you could fillet the next fish you caught. His eyes twinkled as he said, "Well, you never know what you might get if you've been a good girl." I scowled at him and said, "Santa only brings gifts that he thinks are age-appropriate and a knife for a seven-year-old girl is probably not on that list."

Of course, now I wish I'd gotten you that knife for that last proper Christmas rather than the ridiculous Camille doll. I picked her because she was the doll that loved the water so much she was almost a mermaid. Camille even had a pair of turquoise wellie boots like yours. You still wear your boots, but Camille was abandoned the day after Christmas. You told me you thought mermaids were sad, and you just wanted to play on the tire swing your grandfather had hung beneath the old oak tree. I imagine her still propped on your windowsill, watching the dust motes having a disco above your bed.

You groan beneath our tent, and the tent of your rib cage frightens me. I can see each bone-like branch growing away from a delicate trunk, a tree that won't survive another storm. We must eat today. I pivot away from this thinking and decide to leave you in your dreamscape, hoping that it is of a happier time, a time before we all became dusty roadside tramps running from the virus and each other. My father promised he would go into the hospital when his eyes started to turn yellow; instead, he went out into the mangroves with his filleting knife and gutted himself. We buried him under the oak tree where you had spent so much time spinning like a falling leaf. The Spanish moss hung like crepe and cast shadows even on that overcast day as I whispered my gratitude to him. He had taught me how to hunt and fish, and I hoped his words would act like a chain securing us to this world.

When men with hollow eyes started knocking at our door, I decided to leave and head into the swamp. I thought we could forage for food, and I could keep you safe. But the virus is a creature that outstrips any nightmare. It doesn't just affect us; it has killed all the animals and fish. The only survivors are the insects; without any natural predators left, they have thrived.

I scoop up your old birthday cap, it is frayed and grimy, and head out into the cool dawn; it's the best time to catch grasshoppers before their bodies wake up in the sun. When I bring back my jeweled offerings, your eyes stretch wide in an unspoken question. Then, as I light a fire and roast the small bodies, I tell you we will go home soon, a little lie as no one has a home anymore, and then we will use them for bait. But for now, as the burnt orange sun rises, we will crunch them in our mouths, pulling their legs from between our teeth, feeling blessed not to starve today. And I wonder if it might be the small things that save us after all.

Adele Evershed

 Adele Evershed is a teacher who is gradually starting to call herself someone who writes. She was born in a small town in South Wales and now lives in a small town in Connecticut. The towns have absolutely nothing in common apart from Adele and lots of trees. She started her writing journey by producing corny rhyming couplets and scripts for a British expat's annual Panto. This is a peculiarly British type of entertainment that relies on double entendres, men dressed as women and women in short shorts acting the role of principal boy. Since then she has had poetry (of the non-rhyming sort) and prose published in a number of online journals and print anthologies. She still writes Panto scripts and you can see the productions on YouTube if you search The British Theatre Group of Darien. Adele has recently been nominated for the Pushcart Prize for poetry. Her writing can be found at thelithag.com.

The Outing
By Alan Gartenhaus

Café Pierre looked like an old country cottage, with French doors that opened onto the sidewalk. Jayson walked toward it, telling himself to continue past if he felt uncomfortable. He had assumed the bar would be clandestine; like speakeasies he'd seen in movies. He never suspected that it would be quaint, or so public.

He'd only learned of the place a few days ago. Friends had made snide comments. None of them knew about him, of course. No one did. He'd never said anything to anyone.

Jayson had been told that those "afflicted" were sinful, depraved, and dangerous...and while he didn't think of himself like that, he understood that others would. He had no one to confide in, and no role models to consult. His parents referred to such people as abominations.

Standing in the doorway, he peered into the bar's dimness. A heavy-set man wearing a straw boater played the piano. A hurricane lamp glowed on the piano's closed lid, its soft light complementing what seemed a relaxed atmosphere. When Jayson stepped forward to get a better look inside, an elderly, hollow-cheeked waiter greeted him, and with the sweep of a bony brown hand, invited him to sit wherever he wished. Jayson threaded a path to the other side of the room, as far from the open doors as possible.

He fixed his gaze on the gas fireplace that flickered nearby and the liquor bottles behind the bar, glinting like Christmas ornaments. He understood that simply being there had momentous consequences, although exactly what they were remained a mystery.

A different waiter, this one dressed in a white jacket and bowtie, approached his table. "What may I get you?"

Jayson glanced at a hand-lettered chalkboard touting several cocktails as specialties of the house. "I'll have one of your Coco Locos, please." He liked the name.

"Just to let you know, there's a cover charge. It includes a second drink."

"Do I order both now?"

The waiter chuckled. "No. You can wait." He set a

few cocktail napkins on the table before turning toward
the bar.

Though tempted to ask how much the cover charge
would be, Jayson knew it wouldn't matter. He would
stay, regardless. He took a few deep breaths and blotted
the rivulets of perspiration rolling down his sideburns
with one of the napkins. When the waiter returned with
an oversized ceramic coconut shell adorned with a
pineapple slice, a cherry, and mint sprigs, Jayson
laughed, embarrassed by its appearance. "It's more
potent than it looks," the waiter said with a smile.

Jayson tapped his fingers to the spirited piano music.
The piece sounded familiar, jazzy...fun! The type of tune
with witty rhyming lyrics. He listened while pulling
swallows of the frothy cocktail through its colorful straw,
the taste sweet, like a coconut cream pie.

As he sipped, he wondered how a romantic
encounter gets initiated here. Would someone approach
and offer to buy him a drink? He couldn't imagine being
bold enough to take such an initiative, worried that it
could get him punched in the nose. He had a crush on a
guy who lived in his neighborhood...dark hair, sapphire-

blue eyes...but could barely speak in his presence.

The waiter slowed the next time he walked by. "Ready for that second one?" he asked. Jayson nodded. "The same?" Jayson smiled in reply. He felt a lessening of tension in his neck and back, along with something akin to mild sleepiness, the sensation quite pleasant.

When the second drink arrived, Jayson told himself to go slow, but the sultry evening air and nervousness defeated that. Curiosity got the better of him, too; he looked around, surveying the other customers. Everyone seemed rather sedate. He saw no cross-table talk, so when a good-looking fellow at the table next to his leaned over and said, "He's great, isn't he?" Jayson was taken by surprise.

"Who is?" Jayson asked, his heart beating faster.

"Milo, the man on the piano."

"Oh, yes. He's good."

"Good? He's one of the best."

At that moment, the waiter returned and set a glass of water in front of Jayson. "Thought you might want some of this." He gave Jayson a cautionary look.

Ignoring the waiter's suggestion, and concerned that

the intrusion might derail his conversation, he turned toward the man beside him and said, "Guess you've been here before."

"I always try to come when Milo plays. It's not often you get to hear someone so accomplished. Isn't that why you're here?"

Jayson took a swig of his cocktail. He felt lightheaded. "And to meet someone." He couldn't believe that he'd just said aloud what he'd been thinking all night.

The man smiled and turned his attention to his straight-up martini.

Jayson extended his hand. "I'm Jayson."

"Hi, Jayson. I'm Bill. So, who are you here to meet?"

Jayson took another swallow of his Coco Loco. "How about you?" He thought his response clever.

"My wife," the guy said. "She'll be walking in any minute."

"You're wife? You're married?"

The fellow retrieved the olive from his martini and ate it. "Six years now."

The alcohol had overwhelmed Jayson's restraint.

"And she doesn't mind going to a gay bar?"

The man's eyes widened. "A gay bar?" He shook his head. "You're thinking of Café Pierre in Exile. This is Café Pierre. That bar is a couple blocks further down the street."

Jayson's face grew flush. He nodded, settled back in his chair, and listened to the pianist sing Gershwin's "They Can't Take That Away from Me". Instead of requesting the check on the waiter's next pass, he asked for a ginger ale. This evening, he decided, had been a dress rehearsal. He might not be going to that other bar tonight, but he would someday soon. Maybe even tomorrow.

Alan Gartenhaus

Alan Gartenhaus served as an educator at the New Orleans Museum of Art and Smithsonian Institution, and as a director of Cornish College of the Arts, in Seattle. A recipient of an Alden B. Dow Creativity Fellowship, he created and was the publishing editor of The Docent Educator magazine.

His fiction has appeared in numerous literary journals, including Broad River Review, Entropy Magazine, Euphony Journal (University of Chicago), Ignatian Literary Magazine (University of San Francisco), and the Santa Fe Literary Re- view. His non-fiction has been published by Running Press, Smithsonian Press, and the Writer's Workshop Review.

His new novel, Balsamic Moon, is being released in the late fall of 2022.

Between Heaven and Earth
By Joanne Guidoccio

April 2009

Head angel Mark's gaze lingered on the bottle of Johnnie Walker Scotch whiskey. Tempted to have a second drink, he decided he couldn't risk it. Not today. Not ever. Tearing his gaze away from the Scotch, he headed toward the East Wing. As he neared his destination, he struggled to recall the details of his last conversation with the Frugalista angel, but nothing came to mind. Definitely a good sign. If he couldn't remember, then no inappropriate comment had been made.

He found Frugalista reading in her usual corner. "Greetings. It has been a while since we last spoke."

"Um...hmm," Frugalista paused for a fraction of a second, "Seventy-one years, three months, and seven days."

Mark started to question her numbers but quickly changed his mind. How could he argue with such precision? "These are difficult times. The first- and second-tier angels are burning out and refusing to take on new assignments. HE is not pleased."

Frugalista tsked, "If those humans don't change their ways, it will get worse."

"I've had to send in third-tier angels, and the results have been disastrous. They can't handle this economic tsunami." Images of the lingering after-effects of the 2008 recession flooded his consciousness. Layoffs. Home foreclosures. Longer lines at food banks. "I need your help."

"I retired at the end of the Depression and made it clear I could no longer help in the trenches. I spent one decade training two tiers of angels, and they trained a third tier. Even if a few are burning out, millions of third-tier angels are still willing to help."

"They may be willing, but that third tier cannot help. There have been several aborted attempts, and I had to send in first and second tier angels to do damage control."

"You want me to retrain the third tier?"

"No, I want you to inspire and motivate the first and second tiers. We have enough of them to do the job, but they are burning out."

Frugalista gasped. "You want me to retrain both tiers?"

"No, I want you to get back in the field and work your miracles."

Her book fell to the floor, "This…this is beyond me, Mark."

"It's been over seventy years since you walked the Earth. Many angels don't know or have forgotten what you are capable of." He raised his voice. "You read, meditate, and isolate yourself from the others. When was the last time you left your comfort zone?"

"Are you taking me to task?"

"As head angel, I have the right."

"So, now you are pulling rank?"

Mark sighed, "You once performed miracles."

"I only laid the groundwork. Those humans created their own miracles. I don't know if I can…"

"Are you afraid of failing?"

"Failure has never been an option for me," Frugalista kept her voice steady. "If I go down there, I will be successful."

"It is settled. You will go."

"But it has to be on my terms."

"What are your terms?"

"I will assume only one form. I have no intention of reinventing myself to fit each situation. And I will focus only on women over fifty."

Mark chuckled. "Not too many humans or angels, for that matter, can get away with age and sex discrimination.

"I haven't been a total ostrich," Frugalista lowered her voice. "I know what's going on down there. A lot of humans are hurting, but I can't help everyone. I feel a kinship and sympathy for older women, many of whom have become invisible and most vulnerable to the changing economic scene."

"You identify with those invisible women?"

"I don't give too much advice anymore," Frugalista's voice faltered. "No one asks or wants to know what I think."

Speechless, Mark struggled to organize his thoughts. He had not expected to hear such a frank confession from the Frugalista angel. And to think he had stayed away for over seven decades! As the silence grew, he searched for the right words, but none came to mind. He pivoted and asked, "Will you assume the form of a grandmother?"

"No, I will be a fifty-eight-year-old single woman flush with money. Most of these women are divorced or widowed and need to connect with a positive role model," She paused. "All I need is one afternoon, and you will see results."

"In the past, you spent at least a month with each of your charges."

"I repeat...all I need is one afternoon."

Mark started to speak and then stopped. Despite her earlier protests, Frugalista was warming up to the idea. And much to his surprise, he was also enjoying the conversation. "Very well then. Have you chosen a human name?"

"Angelica. Angelica DiMarco."

"I'm flattered."

"Don't let it go to your head. I like the name Angelica. As for DiMarco...it flows well."

***

Angelica smiled as she glanced down at her outfit.

She had taken it from the pages of a fashion magazine...skinny black jeans topped by a fringe black tunic and a long, chunky silver chain. On her own, she added an animal print wool jacket.

She dialed Mark's extension as she struggled with the small phone. It didn't feel secure enough, but according to Mark, the iPhone 3G was one of the bigger models and top of the line. When she asked its price, he had muttered something about high resolution and then changed the subject.

"Greetings, Frug...Angelica," Mark chuckled. "You are in top form. Those jeans are...er...stunning. I've never seen you in denim before."

Angelica laughed. "First time for everything. As you said, I need to get out of my comfort zone."

"I trust you found the accommodations suitable."

"More than suitable." In the past, she had scooted back to heaven after each intervention and taken time to rest and re-energize. But that was no longer the norm. At one of their meetings, the Head Angels decided that more interaction with humans was required. And somehow, that had translated into five-star hotels and luxury vehicles.

Angelica reluctantly agreed to the upgrades but found it difficult to relax in her luxurious surroundings. Dollar signs popped up continuously as she examined each upgrade. She did, however, enjoy driving the Lexus that had been provided.

Mark cleared his throat, "Your first assignment is Greta Bannerman. I take it you have read her bio."

"She has a lot on her plate...job termination, no husband, and a cancer diagnosis. There's no mortgage, but there is substantial credit card debt. I don't see much else."

"There isn't much else. She needed that job."

"Do I find her another one? I don't imagine she has too many options."

"You have your work cut out for you. Good luck." Mark hung up.

Angelica groaned. As head angel, Mark didn't hesitate to delegate or slide out of sticky situations.

She got out of her car and walked toward the Starbucks coffee house. Once inside, her eyes traveled around the glittering cave filled with caffeine concoctions and ridiculously high prices. And all those fancy Italian names—Cappuccino, Latte, Mochaccino, Espresso. During the Depression, a small cup of coffee with cream and sugar cost five cents. Not much by today's standards, but a luxury for people who were unemployed or fortunate enough to get work that paid a dollar a day.

As Angelica moved closer to the counter, she heard the couple in front of her place an order for a Skinny Mocha, Cinnamon Dolce Latte, and two scones. When the cashier rang in their order, it amounted to almost fourteen dollars. Angelica gasped as she recalled several proud factory workers who considered themselves fortunate to receive fifteen dollars a week. She couldn't imagine spending the lion's share of a Depression salary on coffee and sweets. *No wonder these humans are up to their eyeballs in debt.*

Angelica moved to the counter and ordered a Caffè Latte. Approaching Greta, she took note of the frown on the younger woman's face and the book she held in her hands. "Do you mind if I join you? I need a few minutes to drink my latte, and then I'll be off."

Greta looked up. Her short, brown hair was tousled, and red-rimmed eyes dominated her small, elfin face. On a good day, her chocolate brown eyes would light up and animate her features. But not today. Greta shrugged as she lowered her eyes to her book. "Sure, why not."

Angelica took off her jacket and started drinking her latte. After a few sips, she realized what all the fuss was about. While she had always appreciated a hot cup of coffee, she found this new concoction delightful. And despite its inflated price, she might indulge again. She waited a few minutes before speaking. "When were you diagnosed?"

"What do you mean?" Greta's voice trembled with emotion.

Angelica pointed to Susan Love's Breast Book. "No one reads that book for pleasure."

"I picked it up today, but I can't bring myself to take it home."

"It's nice to be surrounded by people," Angelica said as she gave Greta an encouraging smile. "You shouldn't have to deal with a cancer diagnosis on your own."

"Not everyone has a husband or siblings or..." Tears

welled up in Greta's eyes.

Angelica squeezed Greta's hand. "Why don't you tell me about it?"

"Why? I don't imagine someone like you has ever had any real problems," Greta pulled away. "Finish your latte and leave."

It had been a long time since a human had rebuffed her efforts. Angelica could come up with only one example, and even then, the tone had been less belligerent than Greta's. The young widow with four children was devastated when she received an eviction notice three months after her husband's death. And she had spoken sharply to the angel who appeared at her side.

Angelica hoped to get through her first intervention without revealing her true identity. She knew that HE wanted humans to think of angel work as acts of human kindness. For centuries, Angelica had been able to honor His wishes and could count on the fingers of one hand the number of times she had revealed herself. Primarily to males, alpha males who brandished guns and hid behind false bravado.

"You're right. You don't know me, but I know all about you." Angelica took out a BlackBerry, another one of Mark's gadgets, and fiddled with the keypad. When she asked Mark why one device couldn't perform all tasks, he mumbled something about keeping human and Angel interactions separate. The iPhone 3G was reserved exclusively for conversations with Head Angels, while the BlackBerry served as a human interface. Whatever that meant, Angelica thought as she flashed the screen, displaying a heated argument between Greta and her husband.

Greta started shaking. "How…where did you get that?"

"This was beamed to me from on high."

"Now you're an angel. What's next?"

"I'm the Frugalista angel, and I'm here to help you get your life back on track. You've been praying for help and…"

"I've been praying for a long time. My husband dumped me for a younger woman, my sisters won't speak to me, and my mother no longer recognizes me. Last week, I lost my job, and yesterday, I received a diagnosis of inflammatory breast cancer. Why now?"

Angelica paused. How could she tell Greta that heaven was backlogged with cases like hers? And that millions of angels were burning out. "You need me. And I'm here to help."

Greta closed the book and placed it on the table. "All right, you win. Fire away with your miracles."

Another difference, this one influenced by all those angel movies and series. *Highway to Heaven. It's a Wonderful Life. Michael. The Preacher's Wife. Teen Angel.* And Angelica's all-time favorite—*Touched by an Angel.* "That's not how it works. I'm here to guide you and help facilitate change."

"Guide you and help facilitate change," Greta mimicked. "You remind me of those bright, bubbly facilitators who think they can inspire and motivate everyone with their perfect lives."

Angelica winced as she recalled the millions of angels she had in-serviced right after the Depression. Had she appeared that smug? Surely, Mark would have brought that to her attention. She forced herself to focus on Greta. "You must tell someone in your immediate circle about your diagnosis."

"There's no one in my life," Greta's face creased with sadness. "My husband left with his bimbo and moved out of the country. We have no children. My mother lives in a lost world, and my sisters have distanced themselves. I have…had work friends."

"It will get easier," Angelica adopted a brisk tone. "Once you get over this initial hurdle and start your treatments, you will feel better. But you need to tell someone, and I think you should start with your sisters. They are family, and they will be there for you."

"We haven't spoken for a while. When our mother was diagnosed with Alzheimer's, we couldn't agree on her care and where she should be living."

"So, you got an unlisted number and cut off all ties."

"I couldn't handle those telephone calls. I would get at least one each day, and it always left me in a distraught state," Tears pooled in the corners of her eyes. "I still keep tabs on my mother. Her next-door neighbor gives me updates. When Mom's condition worsens, I'll drive up there."

"*Your* condition has worsened, and you need to

reach out to your sisters." Angelica rummaged in her large tote and pulled out the flip phone reserved for human use, "Call each sister and let them know about your diagnosis. Oh, and make sure you give them your new phone number." Angelica stood. "I'll spend the next twenty minutes in the self-help section of the bookstore next door."

"You read self-help books?" Greta managed a smile.

"I don't always have the answers, and I like to see how mankind is evolving."

"You're something else…Fruga…what did you say your name was?"

"I am the Frugalista angel, but my earth name is Angelica DiMarco. Enough about me. Make your calls," Angelica's legs shook as she walked toward the bookstore. Without using technology, she would not have succeeded in getting through to Greta. Would she have to use the phones and reveal herself to each woman?

She took several deep breaths to center herself and headed toward the self-help section. She located David Servan-Schreiber's latest book, *Anticancer*, found a comfortable chair, and started reading.

In the past, cancer had signaled the end of life, but thanks to modern medicine, many cancer patients evolved into survivors. As she read, she found herself agreeing with the author's use of both conventional and alternative methods to treat cancer. After speed reading the entire book, she returned to Greta's table.

"What took you so long?" Greta appeared impatient, but there was an air of excitement about her.

Angelica ignored her question, "Tell me about your calls."

"I called and left messages on their machines. Within minutes, Barbara and Janice called back. I hadn't realized I left your phone on. I hope you don't mind."

"No problem. Continue."

"Barbara organized a conference call, so all three of us could speak on the same line." Her mouth curved into a wide smile. "They came up with the most amazing plan. Barbara is a self-employed copywriter. She works out of her home, but she can work anywhere if she has her laptop and internet access. She is coming down on Saturday and spending the next two weeks with me.

That will take us to the beginning of the summer. Janice is a schoolteacher, and she has the summers off. She will spend the entire month of July with me."

"I knew they would come through for you," Angelica paused. "And now to the second order of business."

Greta groaned, "The money. The job."

Angelica drummed her fingers on the table, "I'm relieved you don't have a mortgage, but I am concerned about your credit card debt and lack of savings. How did that happen?"

"After my husband left me, I splurged on clothes, new furniture, and vacations. I racked up debt and depleted my savings. I had a regular income and could keep up with the monthly payments."

"Barely over the minimum payment." Angelica expelled a loud sigh. She still struggled with the idea that almost anyone, even students, could qualify for these cards and then face years of debt payments.

"I didn't care about the future. I lived day-to-day hoping for a lottery win," Color flooded up Greta's neck to her cheeks as she lowered her eyes. "I didn't win the lottery, and I got cancer. How's that for luck?"

"Not very lucky at all. We need to roll up our sleeves and search for a back-door solution."

"A back-door solution. Is that yours or from a self-help book?" Greta teased.

"A little bit of both, I imagine. Now, regarding the back door. Your front doors are all bolted. There is no money coming in, there are monthly expenses and credit card debt to be paid, and your health insurance will run out in two months."

Greta frowned, "I can't see a back door. I can't even see a trap-door window out of this."

"Not to worry. I have a few ideas up my sleeve. First of all, you need to make an appointment and speak to a bank officer. A secured lined of credit may..."

"It took us over twenty years to pay the mortgage off. It's discouraging to start over."

"Unless there is a hidden cache of money or inheritance, I don't think you have a choice." Seventy years ago, she would never have suggested taking on more credit. But Greta's circumstances called for dire measures. And she did have an advantage with the paid-off mortgage. If she didn't spend foolishly, the line of credit could work as a short-term solution.

Greta drained the last of her tea, "No family money. No inheritance. Just me, myself, and I."

Angelica raised her hand to ward off any further arguments, "It's settled. An immediate influx of cash will keep you afloat. In the meantime, you need to start generating income. I think self-employment is your best option."

"How...What can I do?"

"Barbara is a copywriter. Get tips from her when she comes to visit."

Greta sighed, "I'd rather write fiction."

"Copywriting is more lucrative, but there is no reason why you couldn't do both," Angelica took out a pamphlet from her large tote and handed it to Greta. "Take an online writing course. It will provide structure to your days."

"I've always wanted to write, but I never had the time or felt good enough."

"You have the time now. As for feeling good enough, that will come. If you write every day, you will increase your confidence."

"Will I have time for all of this?" Greta asked.

"Your life will revolve around your medical appointments, but it's a good idea to have more balance. Your sisters will provide social support, and the writing will stimulate your mind.

"Will you help me get published?" A speculative gleam appeared in Greta's eyes.

"I've never created miracles for any humans, and I don't intend to start now. If you follow my advice, you will lay a healthy foundation for miracles to occur."

"Will you keep in touch?" Greta asked.

"I won't be your constant companion, but I will give you my email address. We'll reassess the situation after your sisters leave."

"Uh…about what I said earlier. I'm sorry. I didn't think someone like you could ever understand or help me." She rose and hugged Angelica.

An awkward silence followed as Angelica slipped on a pair of oversized sunglasses.

*****

The iPhone 3G vibrated as Angelica reached for her

seat belt. Taken aback by the interruption, she located the phone and relaxed when she saw Mark's smiling face on the screen.

"Outstanding performance!" Mark exclaimed. "All three tiers of angels watched you in action."

"Am I the only angel down here on earth?"

Mark laughed, "I gave them permission to take a break and get long-overdue in-servicing. And talking about in-servicing. We all got a chuckle out of Greta's initial assessment of you. You know, she wasn't far off."

"Very funny, Mark," *So, there had been some smugness.*

"I have a few questions. How did you know the sisters would offer to help Greta?"

"Greta broke off all ties. Barbara and Janice are kinder, gentler souls who were hurt by the estrangement. They wanted an excuse, any excuse to call her."

"And the writing?" Mark asked.

"When I did my research, I discovered she had written a few short stories and poems during her high school and college years. Once she starts writing each day, she will feel a release of pent-up emotions. The courses will also give her access to an online community of friends."

"You broke two of your rules. That surprised us the most."

"Which rules?" Angelica asked.

"You revealed your identity within minutes of meeting Greta. You also asked Greta to keep in touch and then promised to return. You like to achieve closure and move on."

Angelica sighed. "Cancer trumps the rules."

Joanne Guidoccio

In high school, Joanne Guidoccio dabbled in poetry, but it would be over three decades before she entertained the idea of writing as a career. Instead, she listened to her practical Italian side and earned degrees in mathematics and education. She experienced many fulfilling moments as she watched her students develop an appreciation of mathematics. Later, she obtained a post-graduate diploma as a career development practitioner and put that skill set to use in the co-operative education classroom.

In 2008, Joanne took advantage of early retirement and launched a second act as a writer. Her articles and book reviews have appeared in newspapers, magazines, and online. When she tried her hand at fiction, she made reinvention a recurring theme in her novels and short stories.

A member of Crime Writers of Canada, Sisters in Crime, and Women's Fiction Writers Association, Joanne writes cozy mysteries, paranormal romances, and inspirational literature from her home base of Guelph, Ontario.

Website: https://joanneguidoccio.com

Curse of the Cane Man
By Michael Jefferson

Detective Steve Swanson clips the potted gardenia on his desk, then carefully waters it.

Chief Pasquale Puglisi drops a folder on Steve's desk. "Something for you to look into besides domestic scuffles."

Steve opens the folder, gazes curiously at the black and white photograph of a muscular young man with greasy hair, a monobrow, and an uneasy smile, "Was this taken during the Stone Age?"

"Addie doesn't like to have his picture taken," Puglisi says. "My guess, it's from the nineties."

Greying, with sympathetic but tired eyes, Steve, a twenty-three-year veteran, has come to Chestnut Ridge, New Hampshire from New York City, hoping the rest of his career is quiet and uneventful. He's grateful to be working with Puglisi, who is known for giving his men free reign.

Steve also figures that Chestnut Ridge will be a good

place to raise his award-winning flowers. He thumbs through the pages. "I don't see a rap sheet. Just a couple of mild complaints about public urination."

Puglisi answers in the calm and thoughtful manner that has earned him the respect of the locals, who call him Patsy. "Addison Grey is a special guy, a special case. He's been missing for four days, maybe longer. He's in his forties, but he has the mind of a child."

"You think somebody may have taken advantage of him being naive?" Steve asks.

"Possibly. He collects scrap metal, cans, whatever folks leave out. He's a bit of a celebrity around town, always pushing around a shopping cart. Wears a T-shirt and cut-off short pants, even in the winter. He's got tremendous upper body strength, which makes up for his weak legs. He had polio as a kid, so one leg is thinner than the other."

"Does he have any enemies? Maybe someone who harasses him because of his infirmity?"

"Nah! Addie wouldn't harm a flea," Puglisi says. "People in town lookout for him because he's such a sweetheart, always helping old ladies and kids. And from what I hear, he's got a lot of money."

"From collecting scrap metal and cans?"

"He donated ten grand to the Girls and Boys Club last year," Puglisi replies while he studies the plant. "Gardenia?"

"You're getting better at identifying plants, Chief. Any activity on his credit cards or his bank account?"

"No. Start with the complainant, Cosmo Adams. He's Addie's best friend. He collects the carts at Stop and Shop."

"I hope this doesn't make me wish I was still working domestic disturbance cases," Steve jokes.

***

Steve sniffs the carnation in his lapel, grumbling to himself when he spots Cosmo Adams. Adams is wearing tin foil antennas, perhaps thinking it will improve the sound of the MP3 player tucked in his pocket.

Steve carefully taps the bearded, ruffled cart collector on his shoulder.

"Yeah, bro', whas up?"

"I'm Detective Steve Swanson. You filed a missing person's report regarding Addison Grey?"

"Yeah. Four days gone, bro. The blonde-haired magician took him."

"A magician?"

"Yeah, bro. Dude was wearin' a fancy black suit. He had a black cape, you know, like a magician."

"Anything else you can tell me about this man?"

"He had a cane. When he tapped it on the ground, him and Addie disappeared."

"…Like into thin air?"

"Yeah, bro. Poof! You gotta find my friend. He's sick."

"Yeah, I heard he had polio as a child," Steve says.

"No, it's more than that. He went to the doctor recently. He found out he's got leukemia."

***

Steve plops behind his desk, exhaling heavily. He begins raking the dirt in his mini bonsai plant.

Puglisi gives him a sympathetic smile.

"I should have warned you about Cosmo. But I didn't want you to judge him."

"I have no idea what to even make of him. He says Grey was talking to a magician, then they both

disappeared into thin air. He did say Grey just found out
he has leukemia. Maybe he went someplace for
treatment. I'll run it down and let you know."

"Fine. In the meantime, I'm doubling your workload.
I just got a call from Leslie Hensickle, Harvey Hensickle's
grandmother. Harvey's a trucker. She lives at his place
and says he's been missing for three days."

"Sounds like a potential crime wave."

"I'll warn you this time, Steve. Mrs. Hensickle is
several sandwiches short of a picnic."

"Great. I'll bring some tin foil."

***

Steve sits across from Leslie Hensickle in a rickety
rocking chair. Mrs. Hensickle is comfortably ensconced
in a fluffy armchair that's so big it appears it's going to
swallow the spry, petite, eighty-eight-year-old
grandmother.

"Your grandson's truck is still in the driveway."

"I already told Patsy he's missing, not his truck.
Harvey is a diabetic, a sick boy. He barely made it home
in one piece from his trip to Canada. If he doesn't get his
insulin every day, he could go into a coma."

Mrs. Hensickle points to a gnarly table next to the rocking chair with a package of needles on it. "See? He left his supplies."

Steve surveys the table.

"He also left without his keys."

Frowning, Mrs. Hensickle gets testy. "Are you some kind of idiot? He didn't leave on his own. He was taken."

"I'm just trying to establish where he might be. Does he have a wife or a girlfriend? Did he take a delivery job and not tell you? Maybe he's off somewhere vising someone."

Mrs. Hensickle dismisses Steve's comments with a wave of her hand. "He would have told me where he was going. It was the Cane Man. He came and took my grandson away, just like he took my mother in 1962."

"You saw the man who kidnapped your grandson?"

"I saw him in '62 from my bedroom window. He was dressed like a gentleman from Victorian times. My mother was standing in the front yard, talking with him, smiling. It was the first time I'd seen her smile for a year. She had consumption and it was slowly killing her. I came down the stairs to meet the man who seemed to be making my mother happy. I opened the door, and they were both gone."

"What makes you think your grandson is with this man?"

"That's what he does. The Cane Man comes and takes people away. He did it in '47 too; back when I was a teenager."

"I'm sorry, Mrs. Hensickle, but the math isn't right. If the Cane Man was already a grown man in 1947, he'd be almost a hundred years old by now."

"He's been taking people since they built this town."

Steve lets out a heavy sigh.

"I know you don't believe me. I can see it in that face you're making. 'The old biddy's nuts,' that's what you're saying to yourself. Well, you go ask Gail Goodhue."

"Who's that?"

"She's the head librarian. Mousy looking thing but smart. She keeps the town history, including articles about the disappearances around here."

"All right. In the meantime, I'll keep looking for your grandson."

"I told you, the Cane Man's got him. And he's not

done yet."

***

Meeting Gail makes Steve think Mrs. Hensickle was right about one thing. Gail Goodhue is a dowdy-looking middle-aged woman, with orthopedic shoes, large glasses, and pinched features who lets her unkempt hair fall wherever it wants. But Steve tells himself not to judge a book by its cover.

"I see you like flowers," Gail says, pointing at the carnation in his lapel.

"I grow gardenias, roses, daisies, and I cross-pollinate. My roses finished first two years in a row at the Philadelphia Flower Show."

"Really? I've got a blue thumb. Maybe you can show me how to grow a beautiful garden."

"It's a deal," Steve says. "Leslie Hensickle says your our expert on the Cane Man."

Gail flashes a confident smile that says she's all in.

***

Steve gapes at the computer screen as he reads an article, "Arthur Ashton, Curly Quinn, Herbert Love, and Billy Brundage went missing in 2007," he says. "Ashton had muscular dystrophy and Quinn had heart disease."

"We found out later on that Herbert Love had Alzheimer's, and Billy Brundage had liver disease from long-term drug abuse," Gail adds.

"Why would anyone kidnap someone who was terminally ill? They might die before they could get any ransom money."

"No one's ever asked for any," Gail answers.

"'Brundage's parents told police they had seen the Cane Man outside of their home talking with their son prior to his disappearance…' Guess drugs ran in the family…," Steve comments.

"Keep reading."

"'A local legend, the Cane Man supposedly appears every fifteen years in July to claim four victims. In 1992, Hollis Davis, Patricia McKenna, Chris Cleek, and Nelson Varsho went missing, and four other residents vanished in 1977."

Steve looks up at Gail, who displays her best "gotcha" smile.

"Every fifteen years," Gail says. "That's more than a coincidence."

"I like your enthusiasm and your smile, but we have to prove it."

"I've lived here all my life," Gail says. "A lot of kids were scared stiff by stories about the Cane Man. We were told he was a serial killer, a devil, or some sort of creature that hibernated, then woke up every fifteen years to kill people."

"It's too long a period. One person couldn't have done this," Steve notes. "It could be a cult, though. Do you have any newspapers from 1962 and 1947?"

Gail brings Steve two large volumes of news clips. He scans through them.

"He's mentioned in July 1962," Steve notes. "Four people went missing then too, including Mrs. Hensickle's mother."

Steve thumbs through the crumbling pages of the articles from 1947, coming across an editorial piece.

Curse of the Cane Man Continues
By Ben Bierce

Every fifteen years residents tell their children to come home early, businesses close at six on the dot, and police patrols triple. Because every fifteen years during the hazy summer days of July, the "Cane Man," a benevolent-looking blonde-

haired gentleman, swoops in from the ether and makes four

innocent people disappear forever.

Anyone who wasn't living in Chestnut Ridge fifteen years

ago, in 1932, says we are simple country bumpkins afraid of

the boogie man. But we remember the Branch sisters, Viola and

Shirley, sweet septuagenarians with weak hearts, American

Legion Captain Arvin Wurlie, who was battling cancer, and

Cristobal Fuentes, the elementary school's congenial janitor

who had suffered a stroke. On July 8, Arvin took a walk from

which he has yet to return. The Branch sisters were gone when

relatives checked on them on July 12, and Cristobal's wife, Jeni,

came home to find her house empty on July 15.

The police have stated emphatically that there is no Cane

Man, no gang of marauding kidnappers, no devil worshippers

pulling people out of their beds.

We all felt better this year as July passed into its third

week without incident.

Today, four people disappeared all at once.

Simon Splittorff, Jack King, Jarvis Hooper, and George

Victory have vanished. Four heroes with weak hearts, shriveled

lungs, broken backs, or broken minds. Half a dozen people saw

them sitting on the benches next to the war memorial early this afternoon.

Art Tatum has owned the souvenir shop across the street from the war memorial for the past two years. He laughed at the legend of the Cane Man until he saw him today.

"He was wearing a black cape. He had a cane and was thrusting it in the air like a drum major," said Tatum. "It was odd. They weren't broken men anymore. They looked happy like they wanted to go with him. He marched them past the library, past the town hall."

The Cane Man marched Splittorff, King, Hooper, and Victory into oblivion. If you believe in the curse of the Cane Man, then mark your calendar for July 1962, and plan to take a long vacation away from Chestnut Ridge.

"It's an established pattern," Steve says. "But I need to find out who these Cane Men are."

"I'll be happy to keep looking for you," Gail chirps. "It'll be like we're solving a mystery together."

Steve's cheerful cell phone ringtone catches his attention.

"Chief?"

"We have a third missing person. Go to the Incarnation Nursing Home and talk to Buck Buford, the security chief."

"Chief, have you ever heard about the legend of the Cane Man?"

"Local folklore. I've got an open mind, but please don't tell me he's your number one suspect. If he is, then you don't have much time to catch him."

***

Steve approaches the exasperated head of security. The heavyset Black man eyes Steve suspiciously, muttering, "Nice flower." Buford's temperament remains grim as he turns to look at the empty bed in front of them.

Steve notices the nearby wheelchair and oxygen tank.

"I've been here thirteen years. I've never experienced anything like this," Buford says.

A chubby, red-haired nurse holds back her tears, biting her lower lip. "Me neither. I'm so sorry. It's all my fault."

"Don't say that Hope," Buford says defensively.

"Let's not worry about putting the blame on someone," Steve says. "Whose room is this?"

"Pastor Prometheus Jones. The man is eighty-four-years old, nearly blind. He's got arthritis so bad he can't walk. Plus, he's got a weak heart and has to suck oxygen virtually twenty-four-seven."

"Yet he got up and walked out of here," Steve notes.

"I don't know how. Maybe it's the will of God takin' care of one of his own," Buford replies. "What I do know is he can't be without oxygen for more than fifteen minutes."

"Has he had any visitors recently?"

"Nah. He's outlived his kinfolk," Buford answers.

"A man visited him earlier today," Hope interjects.

"Who was it?"

"I don't know. I walked past Pastor Jones' room and they were talking. Pastor Jones was smiling at him. I heard him say, 'That would be nice.'"

"Was this man tall, blonde, wearing a black suit and a cape, and carrying a cane?"

"Yeah, that was him. I recall thinking he was overdressed for this time of year."

"And when you passed by again?"

"That was when I realized Pastor Jones was missing."

***

Gail turns off the lights in the children's room. Only her office light remains on, giving the building an eerie look.

She retreats to her office, smiling at the bouquet of roses Steve delivered after he left. Opening her desk drawer, Gail slips an envelope she has addressed to Steve inside.

She folds her hands in front of herself and waits.

Gail senses someone else is in the library.

An elegantly dressed man holding a cane appears in the doorway.

"I've been waiting for you," she says.

"You have a choice, you know," the man replies.

"No. I'm not like other people. I can't handle pain."

"There is a part of you that wants to be with Detective Swanson. Perhaps you could be happy together for a while."

"I don't want to be a burden."

"Then we should leave now."

Gail follows the Cane Man out of the building.

***

Hoping Gail is still in her office, Steve parks his car

in front of the library.

He sees a tall man standing near the front door. The buildings outside lights reflect off his gold-tipped cane.

Steve rushes toward him, identifying himself.

Gail moves between the two men, who stare intently at each other.

"As a kid going to Catholic School, I used to wonder what the Angel of Death would look like."

"You can keep wondering," the man says.

Steve draws his gun. "Move away from him, Gail."

"No, you don't understand, Steve. I have to go with him."

"You what? This man has killed at least three people."

"Not killed, saved," Gail replies. "And he's going to save me. I have pancreatic cancer. I've got a year, maybe less to live. If I go with him, I can be healthy again."

"That's not possible. He's a killer, not a healer."

Gail takes the man's hand. "This man is giving me, Addison, Prometheus, and Harvey a second chance to live."

"How? Where are you going?"

"I'm going to a better place. I won't be sick anymore!"

The man taps his cane on the pavement.

Gail gives Steve a last optimistic smile. "Thanks for the flowers!"

Gail and the Cane Man's figures begin to fade, disappearing.

***

Chef Pisani drops an envelope on Steve's desk.

"The staff at the library were going through Gail's things and found this envelope. Guess she intended to give it to you before she disappeared."

"Thanks."

"You know, it's been two weeks since anyone's filed a missing person's report."

"It's a shame the last one was Gail's," Steve replies.

"Looks like its case closed," Pisani says as he walks away.

"…For another fifteen years…," Steve says to himself.

Steve sniffs the gardenia on his lapel, hoping its sweet scent will soothe Gail's loss.

Opening the envelope, Steve pulls out a photograph.
He recognizes it as a picture of the Cane Man.

The back of the worn photo reads:

Dr. Roric Armstrong, July 1852.

The envelope also contains a timeworn article.

July 16, 1852

Gallant Doctor Returns

*After two harrowing weeks on the road, in which he
encountered rainstorms, mudslides, highwaymen, and a bevy
of wild animals, Dr. Roric Armstrong returned to Chestnut
Ridge with a supply of life-saving medicine that will quell the
current smallpox epidemic. Unfortunately, during his absence,
his wife, Abigail, eight-year-old daughter Carolyn, and twelve-
year-old daughter, Cheyenne, perished. His beloved 15-year-old
son, Cain, also died, drawing his last breath as Dr. Armstrong
sat by his bedside.*

*Dr. Armstrong, who has investigated immortality, has
said he will devote his life to healing the sick.*

Michael Jefferson

Michael Jefferson has been writing books, articles, short stories, and scripts since he was 12. His first novel, *Horndog: Forty Years of Losing at the Dating Game* was published in 2017. He is author of more than forty short stories in virtually every genre. His scripts include "Hell in Little Heaven," a western, and "Foul Ground," a baseball treatment.

His second career as a singer led to his writing articles and reviews about numerous artists, including Traffic, Spooky Tooth, The Band, Tony Joe White, Jim Capaldi, and the Moody Blues. His extensive review of Spooky Tooth's "Lost in a Dream" CD is a permanent feature on Goldmine Magazine's website. He was the primary reviewer and writer for Coffeerooms.com for a decade, penning over 80 DVD and 120 CD reviews.

A former amateur boxer, he was 11-0 with 11 knockouts. An avid softball player, he played leftfield for numerous teams for 35 years.

An American in Paris
By Rosemarie S. Perry

No reservation – No problem – Sort of…

Tourist Tales from a Brothel and Other
Adventures

The year was 1972, August. Celebrating a master's
degree I boarded a Russian airline, Aeroflot, from
Pittsburgh to Brussels via Reykjavik for a month-long
European adventure before beginning my new dream job
in Atlanta. This was way before the days of Euros,
cellphones, the internet, GPS, credit cards, and ATM's.

A fellow master's candidate was supposed to join
me. But she bailed at the last minute – a boyfriend issue.
Undaunted, I went alone with a suitcase, a camera, a
round trip plane ticket, some travelers' cheques, and a
Eurail pass valid for thirty days. Unfortunately, I left my
common sense at home. Being an only child, I couldn't
believe my widowed mother let me go alone. But that's
another story.

On the aircraft, I was assigned a window seat. Two

young Russian men were seated in the same row. One decided it would be fun to sexually harass me. I was awakened from a nap when I felt a hand over my breast under my t-shirt. When I complained to the stewardess, she believed them when they spoke to her in Russian, *"Crazy American."* I had to stay in my seat and fight them off the entire flight. My pleas for help were ignored by the other airline attendants. I became vicious to protect myself. I'm sure passengers sitting nearby heard my distress. The men threatened to have me arrested upon arrival. I was too angry to be frightened. As we exited the aircraft, the obnoxious seatmate didn't dare acknowledge his bruises, poor thing... I observed him limping off the aircraft accompanied by the chuckles of his traveling companion. In Reykjavik I insisted on a seat change for the final leg of the trip to Brussels. I noticed the pair did not reboard. Oh, the story gets better...

In the Brussels airport, I exchanged a traveler's cheque for Belgian francs. There I met three American students from New Hampshire, a newly married couple and their best man. The couple were lovely. Their travel companion was a special kind of weird. He talked to plants, said they were his best friends and understood him completely. I gratefully accepted the offer to travel with them, while ignoring the best man's effusive attention to flowering plants. Hey, I was already traumatized by the Russians and figured plants and their friends were pretty safe. The four of us traveled through Switzerland and Italy where I exchanged Belgian francs to Swiss francs and then into Italian lira. We parted ways in Bari as they made their way to Dubrovnik. I hoped my male traveling companion found his true love among the Croatian flora.

I traveled to the Eternal City and reveled in the antiquities, including tossing coins into the Trevi Fountain which supposedly guarantees a return to Rome. What a surprise to see the Coliseum, site of gladiator battles, next to a main street besieged with seemingly hundreds of tiny Italian vehicles.

Upon leaving Rome, I met a female Canadian student on the train to Naples. We became friends and decided to travel together. Exiting the train, we were approached by two American servicemen stationed there. They explained that they were not permitted to date local girls who might be spies. Perhaps they were in special military operations. The soldiers offered to take us to their apartment and showed us around Naples. Complete gentlemen, really. We went to a carnival where we sampled Napolitano street-food. The next day we boarded a ferry to the Isle of Capri where the water's edge is covered with smooth white rocks not sand. Upon our return to Naples that evening, my traveling companion had her way with one of the servicemen. I was content to sleep on the couch alone. No problem. At the end of the weekend, our dates kissed us good-bye at the train station. Bet they still tell tales about the many women they probably met at the train station…

My Canadian companion and I parted ways. Alone again, I traveled to Pompeii (bought ancient Roman glass earrings), Venice and Murano (I still have a vase I bought there), up through the great wineries of Tuscany to Florence where I was moved to tears at the foot of Michelangelo's *David* at the Accademia Gallery. However, nothing could have prepared me for the experience at the Uffizi Gallery.

While there, cognizant of my quickly dwindling

money, I surreptitiously blended into a group with a docent without paying the fee, thinking no one would notice. After reveling in the midst of so many famous paintings, including the *Birth of Venus* by Botticelli, our elderly docent stopped beside another Botticelli painting. He started talking and then stopped, pointed into the group and exclaimed, "A Botticelli! A Botticelli!" Everyone turned around to see the object of his attention, including me, who was trying to be invisible in the back of the group.

The docent came to me and took my elbow leading me from the group. *Oh, great*, I thought. *Another adventure to tell my friends – getting ejected from the Uffizi for non-payment of docent.* He escorted me to stand next to him at the painting and continued talking about the painting. I was distracted hearing gasps from the group staring at us. *What are they looking at? Did that cappuccino stain my top? Did I forget to zip up my jeans?*

The docent continued his lecture while gesturing to the figures in the painting. When I finally looked up at the Botticelli work, I saw an exact likeness of myself in 15th century dress. She had big green eyes and auburn wavy hair. Even her hands looked like mine. I felt faint. Eventually the group moved on, but I was frozen to the spot.

Being of Croatian descent, (Croatia lies 230 miles as the crow flies across the Adriatic from Italy), I wondered, *was this some ancestor whose genes I carried? Or could this be a doppelganger or maybe proof of reincarnation?* Unfortunately, using a camera in the museum was not allowed at that time After a trip to the restroom to splash water on my face and regroup, I went to the museum gift shop and looked through their many books on Renaissance paintings. That particular painting was not in any of them. Upon my return home, I went to the library attempting to find a picture of that piece, but to no avail. If there were not so many witnesses, I would have thought this experience was just really a dream.

The next day I boarded a train to Milan—home of *The Last Supper* as well as Gucci, Prada, Dolce and Gabbana and other designers. Alas, no souvenirs here. I traveled further north through the Lakes Region (a secret heaven) where the snowy peaks of Switzerland tease tourists across Lake Como sweltering in the summer

Italian heat.

It was time to change Italian lira to French francs and hop a train to the "City of Light." Before leaving the states, I had been in touch with a sorority sister who took a job in Paris and invited me to visit. A week before my trip I called her mother to make sure my friend was expecting me and the date of my arrival at her place. Her apartment was near the Louvre. But when I arrived, she was no longer living there! The new tenant had no idea of her new address. By now it was afternoon. Disappointed and ruminating on Plan B, I decided to distract myself and take in the Louvre. Stopping for a few moments at the *Mona Lisa* (*Ciao Bella!*), I wandered through the treasures exiting the museum at closing time. Outside I purchased some peaches from a street vendor. Lugging my teetering suitcase supported by two tiny wheels, I began a search for accommodations. Unfortunately, it seems all of Europe goes on holiday in August. Who knew?

As the sun was setting, I found myself in a little alley near the museum. It was lined with small hotels or pensions. I went to every single one, on each side of the alley. All had signs posted No Vacancy. At the end of the alley, my last hope, I entered the tiny lobby and rang the bell. On the left side, the proprietor had an apartment. At the ringing of the call bell, she opened the half door and we spoke in my broken French. I explained that I was meeting friends in the morning, (a lie), and that I needed a room just for the night. She looked me up and down, as if evaluating my story before leading me to the second floor. I knew from reading Frommer's <u>Europe on Ten Dollars a Day</u> that a tourist should always ask to see the room before paying. Otherwise, the proprietor might take the money and escort the tourist out the back door. I thought it a bit strange that the proprietor would be an elderly lady holding a huge long haired orange tabby. The woman had flaming red hair and sparkly eye shadow. But, hey, this was Paris! I gladly accepted the room key.

Totally exhausted from my predicament and the abnormally high temperatures that day, I flopped onto the king size bed, which was partially covered with mounds of pillows. Looking up I noticed a bed sized mirror on the ceiling. *Hmmm...* Another mirror covered

the entire adjacent wall. Although this room had a sink
and a bidet, I supposed the shared bathroom was at the
end of the hall. *How European,* I thought. Near the
window was a Queen Anne chair with rose brocade
tapestry. The view from the window with lace curtains
was an air passageway – I could see into three other
buildings. Finally, it struck me that this was a most
unusual hotel, certainly different from the American ones
I had visited in the past. I took off my jeans planning to
get comfortable and maybe read a guidebook. When I
went to lock the door, there was no deadbolt or a way to
secure the room from the inside. *What???*

I could lock the door from inside with my key, but
anyone on the other side could circumvent my efforts at
safety with a master key. Too tired to worry about one
other thing, I pushed the Queen Anne chair against the
door and promptly fell asleep.

I was awakened by noises in an adjacent room.
"Thud, thud, thud," was the sound that shook the mirror
on the wall. *What on earth?* I went to the window for
some air and I saw a man and a woman in the building
that was catty corner to mine. They were arguing.

Intrigued, I grabbed my conversational French book. The Frommer's guide neglected to warn tourists that cuss words didn't appear in French conversation books. I couldn't figure out what they were yelling about, although I did recognize a few sexual expletives from crossing the street in Paris traffic. Eventually, the arguing subsided, and all was quiet.

Finally, a thought occurred... OMG – the lady with sparkly eye shadow, the sounds from the adjacent room, the mirrors on the ceiling and the wall, the arguing outside my window, the door with no inside lock and no phone... I was in a BROTHEL! Stupid American! And I was all alone. No one in the entire world knew where I was. The hour was very late, and it would have been really foolish to venture out alone at night lugging a suitcase. There was no way to get in touch with anyone or with the police. And I was exhausted and terrified!!!

Around 2:00 AM, I was awakened by voices outside my door. I slid from my bed and peeked underneath the Queen Anne chair through the bottom of the door. In the dimly lit hallway two men and a woman were facing my door having a discussion. Panicked, I looked for

something to defend myself should they come in and try
to take me away – maybe drug me and sell me off into
slavery. Alas, only three peaches in a plastic bag. I tied a
knot in the bag near the fruit, and kept it by my side… as
if…

Eventually, the trio meandered toward another
room. I heard the door open and shut. Phew, they were
probably negotiating a *ménage a trois* and not coming for
me. My heart was in my throat. I could barely take a
breath.

I returned to bed, clutching my "weapon." Of course,
I couldn't sleep. At the first light of daybreak, I packed
my things and carefully opened the door into the
hallway. Like a feline sleuth, I made my way down the
stairs. The top half of the door to the madam's apartment
was open. She was in a silk robe having coffee with a
gentleman friend. I laid my room key on the door ledge.
She looked up, confused, probably thinking, "Stupid
American." I quickly departed into the gray day. The first
birds were singing. I inhaled and started walking toward
the Louvre. In a more rational moment, I figured perhaps
the room was available from one of her "girls" who was

not working that evening. Rather than lose the entire night's proceeds, the madam decided to rent it to me. Made me smile. A real businesswoman.

On the way through the alley heading back toward the Louvre, I noticed a bar whose proprietor was washing the floor, perhaps just closing up or getting ready for the day. I poked my head into the dimly lit interior. Obviously, I looked horrible. The owner encouraged me to come in and made some coffee for me. A gesture of kindness I've never forgotten.

Although the Louvre was spectacular, I had quite enough of Paris and was happy to depart. A trip to the Eiffel Tower and the Arc de Triomphe would have to wait for another time.

At the train station using my unlimited travel Eurail pass, I departed for Germany and exchanged French francs for Deutsch marks. A high school friend was stationed at Ramstein Air Force Base with her military husband. After walking to their apartment building, I knocked on their door, but there was no answer. I waited on the steps hoping my friends would return soon. As the day wore on, the temperature was dropping by the hour. An elderly woman whose apartment was near the entrance noticed me sitting there. Several hours later, she poked her head out and seemed surprised I was still on the steps with my suitcase. I should have been working on Plan B or Plan C, but this traumatized young person was completely unable to think clearly about solving my dilemma. After dusk, the curious lady came to me and in broken German I told her I was there to visit my American friends who lived down the hall. After moments of hand gestures, she leaned back with her hands on her ample hips, smiled and said, "Baby commin." My friend was in the army hospital having a baby! There was no way to reach them at the hospital on base.

The angel waved me into her apartment. She had already put sheets on the couch and invited me to stay the night. Neither of us spoke the language of the other. Her kindness felt overwhelming. In the morning, after sharing a traditional German breakfast roll and coffee, she called a neighbor who was taking the train to work to accompany me to the station. The kind neighbor lady gave me money for lunch, unaware I had Deutsch marks barely enough for a cup of coffee.

All I wanted was to return home to the U.S. I had a plane ticket but few Belgian francs. Although my Europass was still in effect, I was horrified to realize due to the frequency of changing currency from one country to another, I had very little money remaining. In the train station, I met two young men from Brussels. They invited me to share dinner. Evidently amused by my predicament, they offered me the opportunity to spend the night at their apartment, since my plane reservation was for the next day. Later, they also tried to assault me, but I was able to convince them not to bother me. I suppose by then I looked unkempt and sounded like someone not to be messed with, a woman teetering on the edge of sanity. I slept on the floor. In the morning one paid taxi fare to take me to the airport, probably grateful I didn't make a scene the previous night in their apartment loud enough for neighbors to call the police.

Once in the airport restroom, I washed my face and did my best to look like an exhausted tourist and not a vagrant with a pouch of various European coins worthless outside of their country of origin. I boarded my flight back to Pittsburgh grateful for other Americans traveling home and the ample airline food served in those days. A gray-haired man sitting in the seat next to me bought me a glass of wine and regaled me with stories of his grandchildren. Promising myself to maintain composure and finally feeling safe, I checked my tears and reveled in the coolness of the wine glass against my cheek.

Upon my return, everyone wanted to know about my solo travels, but I refrained from telling the tale in its entirety for years, thinking surely no one would believe me. I never told my mother. She would never have let me out of her sight again. It has made a great story though, all these fifty years later. Some things you just never forget. Perhaps the gods of the Trevi Fountain finally retrieved the coins I tossed into the fountain in 1972. I am planning to return to Italy this year to find my Renaissance likeness.

Rosemarie S. Perry

Now living in Marietta, Georgia, with Tootsie, a rescue Pomeranian, Rosemarie grew up in Campbell, Ohio, a blue-collar steel community near Youngstown. A second generation American, she's the only child of a WW II disabled veteran. With a BA in Psychology from The Ohio State University and a MS in Counseling from Youngstown State University, she retired after 35 years as an educator, once named Cobb County Counselor of the Year.

Rosemarie is the mother of three children, two of whom are deceased. Her son, a former USAF C-17 pilot, lives with his family in Massachusetts. Friends describe her as a lover of all creatures: furry, feathered, and finned. She is also a certified Zumba instructor and former officer of The Atlanta Writers Club.

She has written two books for young readers, My Dog, Me and A Reindear Tale. An antebellum historical novel, Bitter Sugar, is still searching for that agent hiding in the haystack.

"I live to write. I write to live. Yes, I am a masochist…"

Migrations
By C. E. Reynolds

He arrived in dogwood season, the same afternoon she'd spotted the first returning junco come to feed after a winter in the coves. She was chain smoking Newport menthol kings on the porch, considering should she change out of the Winn Dixie poly blouse and walk to the point for a sunset cocktail or just take it easy, get dinner started, when he halted the old truck right in front of her trailer. Calming Jack's bark, he waved his way onto her porch that day. Admitted he was lost. Needed water for the rusty pick-up's radiator.

This Anglo, she sensed, was different. The only one she'd seen so deep in the reservation not driving a white DOI sedan or garbed in a blue Health Services uniform. The first stranger of any variety Jack had let pass so freely. Too, he didn't have that cocksure swagger of a government-issued man. No, he was searching, or perhaps just wandering, following the breeze. Aside from the matted red beard and freckled skin, she'd seen his look in Eastern Band cousins and old classmates back from Vietnam. Thirty-somethings now who left the rez as horny teenagers to return hazed stoners who'd been taught seven ways to kill but couldn't conjure the energy or intent these days to do more than tend a patch of Easy Buds and maybe a few rows of corn and potatoes.

Next afternoon, he stopped back by, offering a six pack for yesterday's directions. Jack greeted him for a belly rub, didn't bark at all this time. They visited, she and he, got to know each other sharing the beers. She liked his easy way, the bushy beard and army tats, the weed he'd rolled when the six was drunk up. They walked out to the point together, sat in the heath bald, finished down a Smirnoff tenth she'd lifted from Winn Dixie. She told him of the sunset point's history in Cherokee culture, its name *Dough nad agave* – "til we meet again" – a generations-old "goodbye" to the sun. In a few days, he became familiar, then more. Capricious, but dependable, somehow. Expected. Like the mountain wind. He introduced her to Joplin, Hendrix, the Dead. Woke her up some nights in fits of scream. In June he drove to Asheville, returning with lumber to rebuild the trailer's rotting porch.

***

Come an early October morn, he was gone. Stepped over the squeaky floorboards, stashed his trash, gave Jack a sturdy goodbye pat, surreptitiously roll-started the truck. From the rear view, he caught a glance of the trailer disappearing into scarlet dogwood and maple leaves in the false sunrise's incandesce. Jack sitting upright, watching him go. He couldn't have told her why. Just had to leave. It was easier just to leave, save whatever sorry ass explanation he might trip over. Whatever fray she might conjure. Maybe every place was haunted. Maybe the haints lived in his head, would be at the next stop, too. Or, maybe, there was peace he hadn't found yet further north of the 17th parallel. Up there, out there. Somewhere. But not here.

He drove the reservation's Jeep trails, never getting out of second gear, careful not to break an axle, flatten a tire in the deep washouts. Entering federal land, the road improved to macadam so little traversed that kudzu vines encroached beyond its shoulders in jagged advances. Breaking daylight made the enormous carcasses of long dead yellow chestnuts and eroded mountainsides even more grotesque, like God's personal apocalypse on Cherokee country. Descending into the coves, he upshifted, passing the occasional trailer or clapboard homes, their windows dark, yards strewn with toys, cannibalized cars, other sundry projects forgotten but by their incompleteness. By mid-morning, he made the little town of Cherokee, pulled into a small truck stop for fuel, oil and coffee. Glimpsed an elder brown-bagging under the counter. Back on the paved Cherokee four lane, he followed signs towards the new Interstate 40. Dialed up an AM station, snow was expected in the elevations a twangy disc jock announced after spinning a hit. The timing was good. He took the west ramp. Bigger mountains, he'd heard. Maybe Canada. Hell, a five-day bender at a roadside motel'd be a good start. He'd think it over at the first open bar. Think over the perils of having lived too long to die young, of having nowhere to go and every day to get there.

***

In waking she was slowly surprised. Worry, then anger – his gear was gone – melded into a well-acquainted melancholy. Gloom, somehow consoling like a well-worn enemy. She squandered the day in the blues – no-showed work, ripped off the bedsheets, broke into the Jim Beam before noon. As afternoon waned and cooled, she drew herself from the couch, pulled on an old barn coat, pocketed the dwindling fifth and stumbled outside across the porch's broken promise. Jack fell in pace, the two meandered the short walk to *Dough nad agave*. Crouching behind a windbreak boulder, she drew down on the Jim Beam, lit up. Jack stretched his long spine, first dipping his forelegs, then reversing, like a rider-less seesaw. Content, he circled into a ball on the soft humus, backside drawn to her hips for warmth, his nostrils flared toward the north winds. Surely, he could smell them. The seeded clouds. Fall's first snow in the horizon.

She came to rest on her backside, leaned against the boulder, pulled the coat's worn cord collar under her ponytail, rested one cool hand in its flannel pocket, another on Jack's furry neck. For distraction, she studied the familiar shapes of ancient mountaintops, sketched them in her imagination. A buck snorted and wheezed somewhere in the near woods, Jack raised to his hind legs, ears up for a moment, and with a short grunt of his own settled back in. As the sunset's colors waned, the world diminished into skeletal shadows of yellow birch and mountain ash, the ghostly sound of a rambling night breeze searching, too, perhaps, for a place to settle.

Having nodded off, she woke in the diminutive light of a crescent moon. Rising for retreat to the trailer, she staggered for a moment, caught herself. Took a brace from the fifth. Her mind was placid, sleep gently beckoned her back. But first, dinner. She stoked alive a fire in the little stove, put on beans and wild onions. Tonight, like too many others, she'd lie alone, still a little hungry, drunk. Morose. Tomorrow, maybe she'd believe again. She always had. Believe as her ancestors in the certainty of hearth and home, the absoluteness of love eternal, in the juncos' return. It was only October, each winter grew longer, each spring shorter. There were dead, she believed, who longed for her, who would have taken her on their passage could they have. Ones to meet again. Migrations to make.

C. E. Reynolds

Ernie Reynolds instructs Creative Writing, Literature and College Composition classes at Florida State University. He is a PhD candidate at FSU and holds an MFA (University of Tampa) and MAT (Belmont University). He has read or published his prize-winning fiction on NPR, the Nashville Review, Writer's Loft, and others.

He is a certified arborist as well as a former garden design/build contractor and former NCAA and professional coach. He splits time between Tallahassee and the Tennessee mountains.

A Night in a Rural Town
By J. R. Reynolds

I was traveling through Texas on my way to meet with some folks in San Antonio when I developed car trouble on the outskirts of a rural town some 60 miles from any major city. I called my insurance company, and they sent a wrecker to rescue me. The driver took me and my car into town and dropped us off at the local Dealership where I was given the bad news that I was going to be a resident of their fair town overnight. They guaranteed to have my car ready by noon the following day.

I asked the Service Manager if he could recommend a good place to stay. He suggested the Continental Hotel just off the Courthouse Square downtown. I was surprised when the Service Manager offered to drive me to the Hotel. He said, "We'll call the Hotel when your car is ready; a driver will pick you up and bring you back to the dealership. It's hard getting around in this town if you don't have a car. There's no taxi service, so car rental or walking is your only options. I didn't think you'd want to rent a car for one day and since it's over a mile to the Continental Hotel I didn't think you wanted to walk. That's also the reason I recommended the Continental, its one block from the Square, easy walking distance to the shops around the Square. There is also a good restaurant and bar next door to the hotel."

Arriving at the hotel I wasn't too impressed with the outward appearance. It was a square stone three story building, but when I entered the Lobby I was nicely surprised. The interior bordered on elegance with comfortable looking leather chairs and murals of what I assumed to be local scenes covering the walls. The receptionist was in uniform wearing a white blouse and blue blazer with the Continental Logo embroidered on the pocket.

As I approached the desk she gave me a radiant smile which seemed to light up the entire lobby, "Hi, my name is Julie. How may I help you Sir?"

"Well, I would like a room for one person for one night, please."

"Certainly Sir, I have a room on the second floor

away from the street and at the other end of the hall from the ice machine and elevator. It is one of the quietest rooms in the hotel and it has a king size bed."

"Sound fine, I'll take it. How's the food in the restaurant next door?"

"It's good! I eat lunch there every day and I've never had a bad meal. Ask for Amy to be your waitress, She'll take real good care of you."

I thanked her. As I entered the elevator I thought to myself, 'what is it that makes people in small towns seem to interact more with each other'. I guess the best way to put it is they are friendlier! In Ft. Worth or Dallas, you can't get the time of day from anyone. They won't even make eye contact with you. Here everyone gives a nod or says hello when you pass them on the street. The people in small towns seem to be more aware and caring of the people and things around them.

After checking in I called the people I was to meet in the morning, explained my dilemma and made arrangements to meet them on Saturday. After finishing my phone call, I gathered up my briefcase and went down to have supper at the restaurant next door.

When I arrived, I asked the Hostess if Amy was working this evening and she assured me she was. She led me to a booth and asked me if I wanted anything to drink? "Coffee please, black."

Looking around There was no one else in the restaurant. I could hear voices coming from the other side of the Hostess station so I figured that must be the bar area. Since its six o'clock in the evening, I would think this would be the dinner hour but evidently not unless they drink their dinners.

A pleasant looking young Lady came over to my table and introduced herself as Amy and asked if I had decided what I would like for dinner as she placed a cup of coffee down in front of me?

I placed my order and started to open my briefcase when Amy asked, "Have I waited on you before? I usually have a good memory for people's faces. I don't remember you and yet the Hostess said you ask for me by name."

I laughed, "I am staying next door and Julie, the young lady at the front desk told me to ask for you. She highly recommended your waitressing skills."

"She's my little sister," Amy laughed as she gathered up the menu.

"Now wait a minute," I said with a smile, "are you saying because she's your sister she's just bragging about you, but you're not really that good of a waitress?"

She stopped and gave me a thoughtful look for about the count of ten, "I guess you'll have to make that decision yourself when it comes time to pay the bill." Then with a smile she was gone.

I was just finishing up my paperwork when an older man came into the restaurant. He was wearing faded blue jeans, a checkered shirt under a faded tan Carhart jacket and his boots hadn't seen any polish in quite some time. He sported a battered grey cowboy hat that looked like it had seen many rain and dust storms. The Hostess spoke to him; he nodded and came on into the restaurant.

The old cowboy walked up to my booth and sat down. I nodded to him and finished putting my papers away before speaking. "How are you this evening? My name is Jerry Wilson," as I reached across the table to shake hands.

At that moment Amy came walking up with another cup of coffee and set it down in front of the old cowboy, "Good evening, Carl, Do you want to see a menu or do you already know what you want?"

Evening' Amy, good to see you again. No, I don't think I'll need a menu. You know what kind of food I like. Have the cook fix me up something and I'll be fine. Do you have any of that Strawberry Rhubarb pie tonight? If you do, save me a piece for dessert with vanilla ice cream on the side, please."

"It's your lucky day Carl. They baked four pies just this afternoon. Mr. Wilson would you like a warmup on your coffee?"

"Yes please, thank you Amy."

I looked around the restaurant which was empty except for Carl and I, "Is this usual on a Thursday night or is there something else going on in town tonight?"

"Now days this is normal, but Friday and Saturday nights it gets pretty busy around here. That's why I come to eat on Tuesdays and Thursdays because it's quiet. It didn't use to be this way. Back in the days when the railroad had their repair shops here this town was a ring-tailed cougar on the prowl 24 hours a day, seven days a week. The shops operated 24 hours a day, three shift a day. Rebuilding locomotives and rail cars was hot dirty work and in the summers when it was 110 degrees or more those guys consumed a lot of beer. There was the Locomotive Shop, the Flatcar Shop, the Boxcar shop, and the Truck shop where they rebuilt the axles and wheels and in the early years before the diesel electric locomotives they had The Boiler Shop. The guys from each shop drank in a different bar and the rivalry was strong. Many a men spent Friday or Saturday night in the hoosegow. The railroad had an understanding with the Law that come morning all offenders were turned loose. The Railroad would pay their fines and take it out of the workers' pay on the next payday. They couldn't afford to have the men in jail. They were more important to the railroad to be working. "

"Did you work for the Railroad?" I asked.

"No, my folks had a place outside of town that kept me busy. When I finally left home, I had developed a liking to the open sky and clean air so I worked on a number of ranches being a nursemaid to a lot of cows. I finally got smart and latched on to a place of my own and here I am 30 years later still nursing cows, the only difference is they are my cows."

"Speaking about rivalry," Carl said. "You should have been here when the cowboys came to town and crossed horns with the railroaders. Now that was a real Donnybrook if there ever was one. Unfortunately for the cowboys they had to stay in jail, sometimes for a couple of days, until somebody came along and paid their fines, whereas the railroaders got out the next morning thanks to the railroad."

"When did the railroad come to town?" I asked.

"They started building the repair shops in 1898 and 99. That's when the town's population doubled almost overnight."

"I would guess that Prohibition must have quieted the town down some when it was in effect?"

"No not really, there was always someone who had a still off in the hills and if you wanted something to drink it was pretty easy to find. There were two brothers by the name of Orville and Benson Wrangle who had a farm over east of town. Each brother had homesteaded 160 acres and then they combined the two parcels together and started running cows. One of the brothers got the idea of plowing up 20 acres and putting in a truck garden. They would grow the best vegetables and the sweetest corn you ever tasted. Every Saturday they came to town and set up at the Farmer's Market to sell their produce."

"When they planted their vegetables it wasn't too hard to notice that their vegetable garden consisted of 15 acres of corn and five acres of garden vegetables. There was a vegetable booth out beside C.R. 305 at the head of their driveway which the brother's wives manned and there were always one or two kids hanging around the booth each day. People would stop and buy vegetables and place an order for a bottle or two of Wrangle's moonshine whiskey. They had a reputation for making the smoothest whiskey in the country and the Fed's knew it. They would raid the brothers, but they never found any whiskey or a still."

"Since the Feds were watching them they never kept whiskey around the farmhouse or barns. When the customer placed his order and paid his money, the wives would instruct them to drive down C.R. 305 and count the fence posts. When they got to a certain number they were to stop and get out and look at the base of the fence post there amongst the weeds and they would find what they ordered. Every night the Wrangle's boys would stash whiskey at certain fence posts and tell their mothers where they had put them. Some were north along the road, and some were south. Each night the boys would change the locations of the whiskey, so it was never next to the same post twice."

"The boys from town would come out for their whiskey and then go a mile down the road to Mother Murphy's Boarding House for Single Women. Mother Murphy ran a strict boarding house, and everyone knew the rules. No one wanted to get crossways with Mother Murphy. Her boarding house was four miles from the city limits, so the Town Marshal didn't have any say over what went on out there. Old Sheriff Tom Negus was known to stop by and pay Mother Murphy a visit from time to time, but never in the 10 years she was in operation was he called out there on official business."

"You said she was in business for 10 years what

happened that made her go out of business; the railroad shops were still operating weren't they?"

"Several things I guess, Prohibition ended, the country was growing up and attitudes were changing. The boys still frequented Mother Murphy's but the County and the Civic Leaders were putting pressure on the Sheriff to shut her down and so she decided to close shop and move to town. She opened a Bookstore and Tea Room across the street from the Courthouse. The shop was very successful to the point she was asked to serve on the City Council which she did for a number of years."

"What happened to the brother's Wrangle?"

"Oh, they continued to make whiskey but the market slowly dwindled away and they became their own best customers. When they closed down the still, they threw a great big party and invited the whole town out to the farm to celebrate. I remember it well, or at least part of it, because I got pretty drunk. The party lasted for three days and when everyone left, the brothers gave a bottle to every person who could still walk as a thank you gift for all the years the people had supported them."

"In all the years the Wrangles made whiskey no one ever found their still. I expect that somebody has stumbled over it by now. If it was kids they wouldn't have any idea what it was. They'd probably break it down and haul it to the recycle place to sell for scrap."

It was time for the restaurant to close and Carl and I had finished our Strawberry Rhubarb pie with the vanilla ice cream on the side along with a pot of coffee each. Amy came up to the table and asked once more if we needed anything else and I told her, "Just the check and put Carl's bill on my check too please."

Carl argued but I told him, "Carl I was ready to spend a quiet evening alone with nothing to do and then I met you and I have been amazed with your story. The least I can do for such an interesting evening is pay for your meal."

As we walked to the door I thanked Carl again for an interesting evening and shook his hand as we parted company.

Amy had my bill ready, and I gave her my card. I signed but didn't add on a tip. She glanced at it but never batted an eye.

"Your sister wasn't lying about you being a great waitress, I left your tip on the table. Oh, by the way, what is Carl's last name? In all the time we were talking I never got it."

"Carl? Why it's Wrangle. Carl Wrangle he owns the Hotel next door and most of the land between here and Ft. Worth."

I stood outside the restaurant looking back in through the window as Amy went to bus the table where Carl and I had been seated. Her eyes got big when she saw the $100 dollar bill laying on the table.. She had the same radiant smile on her face that I had seen on her sister earlier.

I smiled to myself as I walked back to the Hotel, "There is something wonderful about small towns. I hope they never lose their uniqueness and charm."

The End

J. R. Reynolds

All his life J. R. Reynolds has been a storyteller. It wasn't until retiring that he started listening to what people were always telling him, that he should put his stories on paper.

For forty years work had him moving every three to four years to different parts of the country. He saw all walks of life, people, events and places which gave him the material for his stories.

A Saturday Night
By Gerald Ryan

The Gang Tac officer smiled as he picked up the sock filled with Tide laundry soap and hit me across the shoulders. "Where's your weapons' stash?"

I shook my head, "What weapons?"

"Don't be dumb," he said and hit me again. The sock filled with soap suds was a favorite "instrument of persuasion" used by officers in the Gang Tactical unit. It hurt like hell but the diffuse nature of the soft sap spread the blow so it didn't leave a bruise. At least on the outside.

"We know all about you and your East Terminal gang." He held out the sock in front of me. "Weapons! Where?"

I groaned. God damned Phil Dehmer and his can of spray paint. A few months back, he decided that our little group of a dozen or so miscreants deserved a name and he settled on "East Terminal", the name for the end of the 75th street bus line at Rainbow Beach. He'd been busy

painting this on the rocks on the 75th street pier, along the
beach wall that ran from 75th to 79th, at the entrance to
more than a few alleys from 71st to 79th, and on the
cement sidewalks in parks all over our part of South
Shore. If he devoted as much time to schoolwork as to his
spray painting endeavors, he would have been on the
honor roll every semester. He also decided he needed a
handle, so he became "Kingfish" which he painted next
to "East Terminal" wherever he could. The word tagging
hadn't been invented yet, so this artwork of Phil's, excuse
me "Kingfish", was just graffiti. Gang graffiti, the Tac
officer decided.

It started out to be a Saturday night like most
Saturday nights. Dave Haney had called on Bill Handler.
They called on Jack Weyn and Phil Dehmer. Then they
called on me. That is how things worked before cell
phones. And using a regular phone, jacking up your
parent's telephone bill, was out of the question. Your
social calendar for any evening was facilitated by using
the "shoe leather express" from friend's house to friend's
house.

With nothing better to do, we went to meet the

Bitters brothers and Goose Meyers at the playground attached to Bryn Mawr grammar school at 73rd and Jeffrey. Over the past few years of contending for ill-defined borders in a changing neighborhood, this was about as far west that was safe in the evening. As long as you were in a group. That's how the whole "East Terminal" thing started.

We never really went anywhere in groups of less than six or seven. The Blackstone Rangers often roamed the streets looking for some unfortunates to beat up on and scare them further east. This was before they had become a true criminal enterprise selling dope and more. Around this time, they were still contending for street power with the Disciples, so it was mostly a night off for them when they roamed through South Shore, indulging in free-for-all fist fights when push actually came to shove. This was before guns were the answer for every difference of opinion or persuasion. It was a more innocent time. Mostly. Sort of.

Our motley crew served more as a deterrent than a show of strength. We knew tougher guys than us who actually looked for trouble with the Rangers when they ventured east. These guys were strong future criminals, fire fighters, or cops who learned strength with their fists as a way of life from their fathers, uncles, and older brothers. We weren't that tough. We depended on their ferocity to maybe scare any roving bands of Rangers looking for trouble, maybe mistaking us as rougher and tougher so they would keep walking or slow them down long enough so we could run and get away from them.

On that cool night in September, we had no real plans. Idle hands, so to speak. Goose had an idea. "Let's go harvesting." We all knew what he meant. It was "Sukkot" that week, the Jewish feast of tabernacles to remember the experience of the Israelites' years of wandering in the desert. Jewish families would build a sukkah in their yards, a hut to be used for eating and entertaining. The sukkah would have three sides and a roof, but still be open to the elements, meaning open to us. It would be filled with fruits and vegetables, sometimes bread and wine, and hung with colorful, red hot chili peppers and tangy lemons to discourage squirrels from nibbling on the offerings. If only they were hung with something to discourage us.

South Shore was a great neighborhood, roughly half Irish-Catholic and half Jewish. We all had Jewish friends. The Jewish girls dated the Gentile boys and the *goyim* girls dated the Jewish boys. We all got along except for that dark, seldom acknowledged undercurrent of anti-Semitism that permeated Western civilization and all of us. It wasn't something that was taught in school, but something we learned almost by osmosis. So, it would be no big deal to steal from a Jewish family's Sukkot shrine.

Being a good Catholic boy, I really wasn't interested in stealing from the huts but not good enough to stop my friends. Jack and I hung around the playground while the rest of our "gang" headed out on their harvesting venture. "Don't drink all the wine if you find any," I yelled. We sat on the swings and scuffed our gym shoes in the ruts worn into the crushed limestone of the playground. We smoked cigarettes and talked about girls while we waited for them to come back. I kept my eyes peeled for any unwanted company that might be sneaking up on us. Once or twice, I thought I saw something in the shadows across the street, but figured it was just my overheated imagination.

In about twenty minutes, our buddies did come back, tearing into the playground chased by two cops on foot that had darted out of the shadows. They were followed by two unmarked squad cars that blew through the wide gates of the playground. Jack and I were so stunned we just sat on the swings and watched the cars screech to a halt in a dusty cloud in front of us. Before I knew it, I was handcuffed, pushed up against one of the cars, and questioned by one of the officers in the Gang Tactical unit. One of the cops yelled out "Who's Kingfish?" Reflex made us all look at Phil Dehmer. He was put in the back of one of the squads for special attention.

The Gang Tactical unit only existed if there were gangs to be tactical about. Phil's graffiti and some recent jumpings and fights had brought them into our neighborhood and given them a new focus: East Terminal. We hadn't realized that we had been the object of their attention for the past month. So, when the call came in about a sukkah hut being vandalized, they were on us in a heartbeat. It didn't matter that "us" shouldn't have included Jack and me who had just stayed in the playground. We were guilty by association and were all

headed to the Grand Crossing police station and lockup.
At the station, we were asked names, addresses, contacts,
phone numbers, and what are stories were. Jack got hit
with the sock again when he told them his full name. We
knew him as Jack, but his legal name was John Weyn.
The cops thought he was being smart with them. John
Wayne? Whack! They finally determined that we weren't
really a gang, that we weren't bent on anti-Semitic
vandalism, that we were just bored and thought we
could sneak some food and maybe wine from the huts.
They called our parents to come get us but we were still
put in lock up.

We emptied our pockets. They kept our wallets but
let us keep our cigarettes and matches if it turned out we
would be there for a while. Like I said, a more innocent
age. Sort of. We were tossed into separate locked rooms
with the rest of the night's guests. My room had several
Blackstone Rangers already inside. They looked up and
said they all wanted a cigarette and did I have any? I
nodded and gave out cigarettes as fast as I could, like I
was dealing cards. Next, they wanted to know if I could
lend them any of the money that they were sure I had

hidden on me somewhere. One of them had pushed me into a corner and was trying to take off my shoes when the door opened.

"Ryan. Your mother's here." This set off a chorus of hoots and hollers. "Mama come to get you, brother?" my new friend asked as he put my shoe back on my foot. His friends all laughed and crooned, "Mama's here, little man. Go on home now." But under their cat calls, I sensed sadness. None of their mamas would be coming. It would be off to the Audy home on Ogden Avenue if no one came to get them before six in the morning.

We'd been escorted into the station through the back way, so this was my first glimpse of the entrance lobby. Behind the wire grill that covered its face, the clock over the glass entrance doors read eleven thirty. It was late, especially for my mom. A long wooden counter separated the desk sergeant's official domain from the florescent-lit, institutional green room that contained several long wooden slatted benches. My mother and my aunt who lived with us rose slowly from one of them and went up to talk to the desk sergeant. They didn't look at me or say a word to me. The desk sergeant motioned me over to the counter. My mother turned and brought her hand from below her waist and slapped me across the face. "Gerald Ryan, don't you ever do this to me again." She hadn't hit me since I was three years old, when she spanked me for I don't remember what. Through blinking and tear-filled eyes, I saw the desk sergeant nod in silent approval. I guess he didn't see a lot of grey-haired widow ladies hold their sons to account in the middle of the police station.

My mom loved me, encouraged me, and did all she could for me. Growing up, she never spoiled me. Not much anyway. My dad died before I was one, so she had raised me. Not alone because our whole family was involved in my upbringing. But it was my mom who raised me. Even though I hadn't really done anything, I felt like shit for bringing her to the police station late that night. For letting her down. It was a long quiet car ride back home.

The next morning, my Uncle Norman was there for breakfast at my mom's request for a little talking to. He told me how bad companions could ruin your life, rattling of the names of so many of his friends who had died or been put in jail. He said my mom was afraid that the friends I was hanging around with would get me in more and more trouble, especially as South Shore changed. Growing up in Canaryville, he knew that to survive in a tough neighborhood, you had to make choices. Some choices that made sense in the spur of the moment could haunt you for the rest of your life. He was here to tell me that I damn sure wasn't going to make them.

Within the month, my mom and I moved from South Shore to live with my other aunt in the western suburbs. I really don't think I would have turned out all that bad if we'd stayed in South Shore. But you never know. My bad companions turned out to be an interesting lot. Kingfish, Phil Dehmer, turned out to be the manager of a small grocery chain. Dave Haney retired from the Navy and started his own consulting business. Bill Bitters and Jon Bitters both became refrigeration mechanics. John Weyn and his family moved to a nearby western suburb shortly after we did. He was Best Man at my wedding. Bill Handler just disappeared. Jim "Goose" Meyers is doing life for murder.

And I turned out just fine. I think.

Thanks, mom.

Gerald Ryan

 In the early 90s, Gerald Ryan enjoyed an unplanned sabbatical from his job and went back to school where he took a writing course. It was like someone let the genie out of the bottle. He hasn't stopped writing since.

He loves cycling. Friends constantly called with cycling questions. The result was a series of articles for the Courier Sun and Windy City Sports in Chicago, the Chicago Amateur Athlete, the Liberty Suburban Chicago Newspapers, Senior Living Magazine, and weekly radio spots for WDCB-FM in Glen Ellyn, IL.

Poetry fills a need that other forms of writing don't, allowing Gerald to stay in emotional touch with feelings and work through life issues. He enjoys the denseness of language and economy of words inherent in a poem. His poetry has appeared in The Prairie Light Review, won the Mountainland Publishing Poetry Grand Prize and received an award in the Fifth International Poetry Contest in the Firstwriter.com Magazine."

In May 2007, St. Martin's Press published his short story "A.K.A." in the anthology, Next Stop Hollywood, Short Stories Bound for the Screen.

"And The Road Goes On Forever, won first place in the Creative Nonfiction contest in the Bacopa Literary Review 2021.

In April, 2022, the poem "Lip Jazz" appeared in the magazine Jerry Jazz Musician.

Dodge City
By Ann Worrel

Rick felt the cold sidewalk beneath his cheek and took in a breath of air that tasted of tar and old rubber and tequila. He opened his eyes and pushed Drew's foot away from his nose. Drew stirred but did not wake up. Rick pulled himself to a sitting position, cupped his hands and dipped them into the still fountain. He splashed the green water over his face.

He had grown up in this park. The tall slide stood about thirty yards away, next to the see-saws and swings. He fell off that slide when he was four and lost his front teeth. They were only baby teeth but somehow the fall had caused his permanent teeth to come in crooked, requiring very painful alignment. He rubbed his eyes and stared at the slide until it came into focus. All of the playground equipment used to be set in cracked, black asphalt surrounded by grass, but now the whole area was covered with small, rounded pebbles as if an ancient mountain had disintegrated there, leaving the rounded rocks to protect little children from hard falls. He fished a cigarette out of his pocket and lit it, drinking in the smoke as though it contained a stronger drug than nicotine.

He stood up a little too fast and sat down again, trying to remember how he had gotten here. Looking around for clues, he spotted the abandoned tequila bottle and the warm, half-empty case of beer next to it. He leaned over and took one of the stale beers, opened it and had a small, tentative sip. "Damn," he whispered, wiping his mouth. "Little hair of the dog never hurt anybody," taking a larger swig, chasing it with a hit on his cigarette. He sat, drinking and smoking and staring at the building across the street. He thought about how he used to play right here in this park every day when he was a kid never once suspecting that the ugly structure opposite him inhaled young men and then spit them out on the shores of a foreign, bloody land.

The day he discovered he had a low draft number, a straight tall officer in green fatigues had pulled little white slips of paper with the days of the year written on them from a large turning canister just like a game show host drawing the grand prize winner for the day.

"Nobody I know has ever won anything in a drawing," Rick joked with Drew as they sat, waiting for news, hoping his words would further reduce his chances, "there's no way I'll get called early." He was wrong. His birthday was the sixth date pulled from the container.

"I guess close is good enough in horseshoes, hand grenades *and* the draft lottery, my friend," Drew cheerfully remarked before either of them had fully understood the consequences of a low number. Damn Drew, anyway. Rick would probably be through with his twelve-month tour before Drew even went to boot camp.

He thought he'd just go. It made him miserable to think about it, but he thought he should go. He'd make it. He'd have friends, he always had friends, just like Drew and the other guys. They'd have some tough scrapes, but hell, they live through them, and then they would talk themselves into oblivious old age with their fine stories of war. Just like the old-World War II guys. Yeah?

Then he met Captain Black. He was a friend of

Drew's mom and lived in the garage apartment behind
her house. He made cabinets during the day and sold
them to a contractor in town. His work was
unremarkable, but consistent. It paid the bills. Rick and
Drew felt compelled to visit him sometimes during the
hot summer evenings. They would sit in the dusty
sunlight that filtered into the room through old yellow
venetian blinds smoking and examining the gold brocade
sofa, the teak end tables and the red Persian rug that
covered the floor while they waited for Captain Black to
speak. It smelled like mothballs and the cigarettes which
Captain Black smoked one after the other.

He would tell them stories about the wars. His
memories of World War II were hazy, sun-drenched,
happy stories of a young man who spent more time
whoring and drinking on its sandy Pacific beaches than
waging war on its battlefields. These stories were filled
with romance and mischief like a summer spent at camp.
He told them one about a young officer who was
dispatched from their ship with two suitcases, one
carrying plans for the invasion of Japan, the other empty.
His top-secret instructions were to ditch the plans with

the correct recipient ASAP and return to the ship with both suitcases full of the best whisky he could get his hands on.

The guerilla wars were different according to Captain Black and his memories of those wars were bloodier, his stories delivered in a clipped language with clenched teeth. He told them about a man in Vietnam who came to them distraught, begging for help for his sick child. When he handed the child to the sergeant in charge, he pulled the pin on the grenade that was strapped to the little girl and ran away while she and the sergeant were blown to bits.

Rick went to see Captain Black the day he learned that he was near the beginning of the line. Captain Black said just what he always said. "Don't go."

"What do you mean don't go? They called me, I gotta go."

"Don't go."

"I can't just not go. I'm thinking about joining the Navy while I still have a chance to choose. They say the Navy's better, unless you get stuck on one of those riverboats. You know anything about those, Captain

Black?" Rick asked, worrying as he did about what kind of story Captain Black would come up with to convince him that the riverboats were indeed the quickest way to a sure death. Visions of "Bridge on the River Kwai," including near starvation and intense brutality began churning in his head.

"Don't go."

"I got bad knees and maybe an ulcer, too. My brother had an ulcer and he didn't have to go. He just told 'em and they called his doctor, and that was it. He was out. Just like that." Rick snapped his fingers to emphasize his point.

"Got a buddy with bad knees."

"Yeah, so? Did he get out too?"

"Got out, all right."

"Okay, see?" Rick said, trying to convince himself and Captain Black, too. "I'll just call up Dr. Turner. He's been my doctor forever. Or maybe my Mom could call him. Anyway, he'll write a note and say I have bad knees or whatever and I'll get out just like that guy you know."

"Made my buddy go," said Captain Black, his lips tightening around his teeth in a grimace.

"Oh?"

"Fixed his knees, free of charge. Sent him back without any. Sits in a chair. Shits in a bag. Plays dominoes. Government sends him to a shrink. Shrink gives him drugs."

Rick didn't know what to do. He didn't want to go to jail, for God's sake. He spent the next few months trying to forget about the whole thing. He quit visiting Captain Black and tried to get more serious about things like water skiing and working at the lakeside resort down the road from his house. Captain Black's voice would come to him from time to time while he was doing something else like washing his car or kissing his girlfriend.

"Don't go," the voice would say and Rick could feel his presence like an unsmiling Cheshire cat. "Don't go. Don't go. Don't go." He heard the words over and over in his head like a silent penetrating mantra. And now here he was in the park, still unsure. He wished he could sleep like Drew and Eddie and Rocky whose bodies littered the pavement. They could sleep anywhere. Eddie had snuggled up next to the beer, his arm wrapped around it as though he were a child cuddling a favorite stuffed animal. Rocky was a few feet beyond, lying on his back, his legs staked wide apart, mouth open, snoring loudly. Rick couldn't decide if they looked like corpses or sleeping babies. Too bad they weren't going...they'd probably be right at home sleeping in a damp foxhole with mortar shells dropping everywhere. And he would sleep a little knowing they were there.

Scenes from last night filtered through his soggy brain as Rick approached the final stages of waking up. They had stopped at Scholz's to admire the sorority girls in attendance for a weekly beer-drinking contest and somehow Rocky had convinced two of them to come along on a skinny-dipping expedition in a fountain on the UT campus. The clock tower on the hill above them glowed orange and the light gave an eerie presence to the scene, like a full harvest moon on Halloween. The fountain was filled with statues of wild horses, running like mad in the orange water. They splashed one another and had chicken fights, the girls straddling Rocky's and Eddie's shoulders and trying to knock one another off. They rolled down the grassy hill until they were too dizzy to stand up and stayed there on the grass for a while trying to identify Orion and Scorpio in the night sky. They wrapped themselves in their clothes and smoked the hash Rick had brought along. They took turns drinking tequila out of the bottle until Drew, with a burst of energy leapt onto the back of one of the racing stallions and shouted "Hombres," as he liked to do when he'd been drinking tequila, "We ride at dawn like the breaking wind. Who's with me? Andale! Arriba!". And he gave a high-pitched yell as though he were leading Pancho Villa himself into battle. Rick ran up and joined him and they yelled and rode the stallions into the black night while Eddie and Rocky necked with the girls on the grass.

Later, they stumbled over to the park and sat on the edge of the fountain. Drinking beers and staring at the bland building with disgust. Some form of retribution seemed to be called for, but no one volunteered any ideas until Drew rallied them. "Hombres!" he shouted, holding the bottle of tequila above his head as though it were a heavy pistol, "we piss together on the grave of your enemy's mother." He gave a war cry and all four of them ran across the street and began peeing on the front steps of the draft board, their urine making dark yellow puddles on the pink granite steps. Rocky was making a cackling laugh like a bandido on mescal and Eddie was swinging a frayed piece of rope like a lariat over his head. Drew started singing in a deep, pious voice. "Glory, glory hallelujah." Then they had all joined in. "Glory, glory hallelujah. His truth we're pissing on."

Now Rick sat, watching the parking lot to the left of the building fill. He watched the workers, some dressed in civilian clothes, some in fatigues and starched khaki uniforms emerge from their cars and disappear into the building. The air was thick with humidity, and it was already warm, the sun having ascended just enough to blind him if he failed to shade his eyes from its glare. He could smell the tar in the newly paved street cooking up. Turning his head, he saw that Drew and Eddie were awake and sharing a joint. Carefully, he picked himself up and sat next to them, extending his hand for his turn. They smoked silently for a little while. Taking the last hit, Rick inhaled and held it in.

Drew asked, "What're you gonna do?"

"Don't know," said Rick, the sweet smoke streaming

from his mouth and nostrils as he spoke. "Guess I'll go in and see what happens."

Rick stood facing Eddie and Drew and Rocky who was still lying on the pavement next to them snoring and raised his beer in mock salute. His long hair was unbrushed and parted in the middle, hanging down chest-length on either side of his face. He had on faded jeans with a hole above the right knee and the hem of one leg unraveling over his desert boot. Over his blue work shirt he wore a vest made from an old black and white striped Mexican blanket with cotton fringe on the bottom. "Here I go," he said with resignation, "give me liberty, or give me..." and he paused trying to think of a catchy conclusion to make them laugh. Drew did it for him.

"Rock and roll!" he yelled and pounded the pavement with his hands like a drum. Rick clicked his heels, turned and began his approach toward the building while Eddie and Drew and even Rocky jumped up pretending to play guitar, dancing and strutting like rock stars and singing "I can't get no satisfaction. I can't get no-o-o-o...." Their voices stopped abruptly as he

entered the sterile government building and the door
closed with a vacuum-packed finality that made Rick feel
as though he had just entered a sealed refrigerator.

"Satisfaction," he concluded with a whisper.

An hour later, Rick had filled out a half-dozen forms
and was still waiting to talk to someone who wasn't
hidden behind a glass partition. He studied the pock
marks in the olive-green tile directly beneath his feet
while he waited. He looked up and caught his reflection
in the glass door to the office a few feet in front of him.
He looked awful and felt pretty bad, too. "Like a wolf ate
me and shit me off a cliff," Drew would've said. He
probably smelled terrible-like two or three smoky bars
and that sweet morning-after old beer smell. Good.
Maybe they'd take one look at him and tell him to get
lost.

"We don't want your kind smellin' up our jungle,
boy. You gotta lotta nerve comin' here to the United
States Army and thinkin' you can get a free ticket to
shoot gooks lookin' like that. No sir, we want only the
cleanest boys goin' over to shoot things up in Viet Nam."
He whispered it out loud, "Vee-yet Nay-am," so that

each vowel was a separate syllable and the last part rhymed with lamb.

"Richard Anderson?" called the well-pressed sergeant from the partially open door of his office.

"Uh-right here," Rick called back from his chair. He crossed the five olive-green tiles toward the sergeant, his movements thick and slow as though he were wading through a swamp filled with molasses and shook the officer's hand. In Rick's fantasy, the sergeant was a snarling, stupid redneck. In reality, he seemed calm and possibly intelligent. "This isn't going to be easy," Rick thought as he tried to get comfortable in the wooden swiveling chair across from the Sergeant. "Don't go," whispered Captain Black from a corner of his subconscious.

"Richard, according to the dope I've got, you consider yourself to be a conscientious objector, is that correct?" he asked courteously.

"Yes sir." Rick found to his disgust, that he was incapable of leaving the "sir" off of his answer to this middle-aged, uniformed gentleman. He imagined Captain Black slapping his forehead and shaking his head at Rick's formality.

"Wonder if you could tell me a little more about this situation of yours, Richard." He sounded genuinely bewildered. "Does your religion specifically prevent your participation in combat?"

"No, sir, I just don't want..."

"Have you been an active member of this religion all your life?"

"I just don't want to..."

"Can you supply legal documents attesting to your continued participation in said religion?"

"I just don't want to kill people I don't even know. I'll be a medic or..."

"Are you prepared to face criminal prosecution in the event that your claims are not substantiated by the United States Army Board of Investigation?"

"A cook. I'm a pretty good cook, you know."

The sergeant took a deep breath and sighed as though he heard this all the time. He looked Rick straight in the eye.

Rick looked back, trying not to squirm under the authoritative stare.

The Sergeant continued with measured exasperation, "son, if I let every recruit who walked through that door and said he didn't want to engage in combat become a cook, I'd have an army full of shivering, whining cooks serving shit to my soldiers. It ain't gonna fly, son." He sat back in his chair and took on a fatherly tone. "Now there's no real hurry on this thing. You look like you could use some rest. You been drinkin', son?"

"Little bit," admitted Rick.

"Why don't you go home, hit the sack and think about this a little more. The Private on duty in the reception area will reschedule for next week," he said, smiling pleasantly.

"Don't go. Don't go. Don't go. Don't go," the chant began, keeping time with Rick's rising pulse.

"I'll be drunk, sir.

"The Sergeant's smile, though still intact, tightened. "Pardon me, son?"

"I said I'll be drunk, sir. I guess I got a drinking problem. I guess I might just be a habitual drunk." Captain Black puffed on his cigarette, nodded and retreated into Rick's subconscious.

"Now listen to me. You are officially a recruit of the United States Army. You are under orders to return to this building at 0800 hours one week from today. If you do not fulfill this obligation, a warrant will be issued for your arrest, and you will become a fugitive. All necessary measures to apprehend and prosecute you will be taken. Do you understand, Recruit?"

"Yeah." Rick was already on his feet and on his way out.

"Oh, and Sergeant?" Rick paused by the door. "I really am a good cook." Rick skittered across the waiting room as though the officer might start hurling books and the framed family photos that littered his desk at him. He paused in the reception area long enough to thumb his nose at the Private on duty and then pushed open the heavy door and breathed in the sunshine.

Across the street, his friends sat solemnly and patiently. Behind them, the playground was full of scurrying children and their anxious mothers. As Rick watched, one small boy climbed slowly to the top of the slide and stood there, teetering on its summit. He called to his mother, "Mommy! Look at me! I'm way up high!"

The boy's mother looked up from her conversation. She smiled and waved and said, "yes, look at you. What a big boy." Rick caught his breath and waited for the inevitable fall and the terrible hurrying that follows such accidents. Instead, the boy turned and slowly lowered himself to a sitting position and finally, with a big push, slid triumphantly down.

"Well?" asked Drew as he crossed the street.

Rick caught the beer that Drew tossed to him, took a long draw on it and wiped his mouth on his sleeve. "Ah guess ah got me a price on my head," he said in his best western drawl.

"Damn, looks like it's Dodge City for you, man. Amigos!!" yelled Drew turning to the others, "we ride at once with our brother. Vamonos!"

The End

Ann Worrel

Ann Worrel is recovering from a long career in the roller coaster world of the oil and gas business where she held management positions with large oil companies. She received her BA in Russian Language and Literature from Vanderbilt University and her Masters in Geology from the University of Texas at Austin. She lives in Houston, Texas with her dog, Foxxy Cleopatra (apologies to the Austin Powers movie franchise) and has rediscovered her love for writing now that her two children are grown.

Ann spends her days writing, reading, working out, attempting to play golf and hosting a cool group of friends for weekly yoga and wine tasting. She travels often and her favorite destinations are the Texas Hill Country, the East Coast and points abroad. Her current writing projects include a work that explores online dating for seniors and a mystery novel set in Key West.

Living Springs Publishers

We hope you enjoyed this book. Please let us know what you think about it. You can leave a review on Goodreads, or wherever you purchased the book.

This is the sixth edition of our Baby Boomers Plus contest and book. The number of submissions to **Stories Through The Ages Baby Boomers Plus** has increased dramatically over the six years we have conducted the contest. Each story is read by at least three judges. We receive stories from people just starting to write and from those who have won many awards. The competition is intense, and the judges agonize over their choice, realizing the heavy burden of being fair but decisive. There are winners and losers, that is the nature of a contest. We thank each and every author for the stories they submit and urge everyone to keep writing.

You can find information about our contests and buy our books at www.LivingSpringsPublishers.com.

Living Springs Publishers is a family owned, independent publishing company based in Centennial, Colorado. Our mission is to help authors, regardless of age or experience, share their gift of writing. Using our expertise in editing and publishing we help our clients bring their stories and manuscripts to life.